ONE DAY IN THE LIFE
OF
MARTY McKENNA

by

Doug McKim

ISBN – 978-1-0881-2028-6

"Guide Me O Thou Great Redeemer"
(Cwm Rhonnda)
Original Lyrics by John Hughes

"A Minstrel Boy" by Thomas More

"Danny Boy" Original Lyrics by Frederic Weatherly
Often Set to the Tune of "Londonderry Air"

"Garry Owen" Traditional, Commonly Adopted by Military Units

Cover Artwork by Jayson Cable ©2013/2023

ONE DAY IN THE LIFE
OF
MARTY McKENNA

*Dedicated to Robby Midgett
Promise me that the glories of the written word
and advent of fine literature
shall never perish!*

1

"Take 'em to Missouri, Matt."
"Yee-haw!"
"Wee-haw!"
"Ahh-haw!"
"Hoo-raw!"
"Eeh-yah!"
"Fuckin' A, awright!" cheered sixteen-year-old Marty McKenna as he sat in the small, narrow bed, in a small, narrow bedroom, in a small, narrow *Fleetwood* trailer, in a small, narrow trailer park, in a small, narrow neighborhood, in a small, narrow section of Grangeford, Oregon.

Grangeford, Oregon ....

Population, fifteen thousand....

Or something like that....

The trailer park was nestled between Interstate 84, with a constant roar of east and westbound traffic, and the tracks of the *Union Pacific Railroad*, with its constant rumble of east and westbound trains. Nearby was a busy turnpike, where travelers headed west toward Pendleton, the Dalles, and Portland, east toward Baker City, Ontario, and Boise, north toward Milton-Freewater, Walla Walla, and Spokane, and south toward John Day, Redmond, and Bend.

Most of the homes in the trailer park were in dire need of repair. Adjoining streets were dusty, dirty, and eroded. Few new automobiles were found in the neighborhood, and were generally more expensive than the houses they sat next to. All carried payments which the owners couldn't afford. A quick trip to bankruptcy, or surprise visit from the repo man. Older cars ran poorly, if at all.

Marty McKenna relaxed in his filthy bedroom, watching a DVD of *Red River* on a crappy DVD player, hooked to an even crappier fifteen-inch, analog TV. Blankets hung from his bed, smeared in muddy footprints.

Marty viewed the classic, black and white Western movie with an intense glare. A can of *Coca-Cola* was in one hand, a *Camel* cigarette in the other. An ashtray, overflowing with cigarette butts, sat next to him on the bed. Occasionally, Marty nibbled on *Western Family* donuts.

Empty pop cans were littered throughout the bedroom. CD cases were scattered upon a lopsided table, next to a worn-out, mini-stereo. Partially eaten bags of potato chips decorated the floor. In one corner of the bedroom, rainwater dripped from the leaky roof into a rusty coffee can. Outside, thunder exploded from the darkened, overcast skies.

Morning.

Marty wore a bright red, hooded sweatshirt of the *Northern Oregon University* Lumberjacks, short-short cutoffs, white socks scrounged around his ankles, and dirty white Adidas. He had unruly, shoulder-length red hair. His face was somewhat freckled, his nose slightly pugged. He had narrow, deep-set blue eyes and a round, cleft chin. His bare legs were sinewy and tanned.

Marty took a drag from his cigarette, sipped his drink, and enjoyed his donuts. Both eyes widened as a wild, enthusiastic grin highlighted his face. He eagerly watched a large group of rough, rugged, and rowdy cowboys begin a perilous journey to move cattle from Texas to Missouri.

Marty was really getting into the movie as someone beat on the panel wall, separating his bedroom from the next. "Shut the fuckin' TV down!" a muffled voice shouted, from behind the flimsy wall.

"Aw, what the fuck ever," sighed Marty, rolling his eyes back. He resented taking orders from Losers of the Month, sorry excuses for men that his mom, E McKenna, brought home from the taverns. The current Loser of the Month, Lance Copperfield, wasn't the worst of the bunch. He for damned sure wasn't the best! No matter. Marty still wanted to slit Lance's throat, then watch him bleed to death in a filthy gutter. Lance had long overstayed his welcome, and needed to leave (or go off somewhere and die).

Water dropped from the ceiling into the coffee can, with an endless, maddening...

Drip, drip, drip...

Drip, drip, drip...

Drip, drip, drip...

"Do us a big favor, Lance," said Marty. "Either keep your goddamn mouth shut, or get the fuck outa our house!"

"Like me to come over there?" growled Lance, from behind the wall. "Turn the fuckin' TV down, or I'm bustin' it over your fuckin' head!"

"Then come over here and make me," whispered Marty, leaning across the bed to manually turn down the TV's volume. "Get your ass over here, loudmouth, so I can *Riverdance* across yer fuckin' head..."

Marty slurped down the last of his Coke, chowed down the last of his donuts, and extinguished his cigarette into the ashtray. He stretched, yawned, scratched his crotch, and glanced at a digital clock radio on the table.

9:53 am.

Marty peeked outside, through a dusty window near his bed. Storm clouds blanketed the city. Rain dampened a thick, overgrown lawn surrounding the Fleetwood. A couple of *Huffy* ten-speed bikes, both with flat tires and rusty chains, leaned against a steel-meshed fence. The ear-shattering whistle of an oncoming train sounded in the distance.

"What the hell?" griped Marty. "More rain? Son of a goddamn motherfuckin' bitch...."

Marty heard a knock on the living room door. Moments later, the door opened, then closed. "Is Marty here?" a familiar voice asked.

"In his room," said Patrick (which Marty referred to as Fatrick). Patrick was Marty's lazy-assed, twelve-year-old brother, who did nothing but play stupid-assed video games all day.

The *clump, clump, clump* of footsteps through the hallway neared Marty's bedroom. Marty grinned, dropped his cutoffs and drawers down to his ankles, then spread his legs.

There was a knock on the bedroom door.

"C'mon in, Kris," smirked Marty.

In walked Kris English. He was a handsome, towheaded kid of sixteen with a fair complexion and a slight build. He stood nearly a foot taller than Marty. He wore a *Levis* jacket, a long-sleeved tee-shirt featuring the mascot of the Grangeford High *Bobcats*, blue jean shorts, clean white socks, and deck shoes. His knees and shins were hairless and pale.

Kris' thoughts as he glanced down upon Marty's exposed genitals were of annoyance, followed by muted attraction, and finally deep-seated guilt, anxiety, and despair.

"Go on, Kris," taunted Marty. "Take a ride on nine inches of eastern Oregon white snake."

Kris quickly turned his head away and gasped. His heart skipped a beat. He was torn between his interest in Marty's nudity, and his strict, God-fearing, Biblical upbringing and values.

"Damn you, Kris," grunted Marty, pulling up his cutoffs as he stood to greet the visitor. "You ain't no fun at all."

"Who says you are?" whined Kris.

"I'm always fun. You woulda found out how much fun had you hopped upon my nine inches."

"More like nine millimeters," sighed Kris, his voice jittery. "Why do you pull that crap on me, Marty? What makes you always pull that crap on me?"

"What crap?" questioned Marty, innocently.

"You know what crap!"

"Because you want it, Kris." Marty grinned. "Admit it, Kris.... You want it."

Kris shook his head in denial.

"Aw, to hell with it then," said Marty. "Tell ya what, Kristoffer.... I'll make it up to ya, and buy ya breakfast!!"

"No, Marty," mumbled Kris, tiredly. "You don't have to buy me breakfast."

"But I want to!" Marty retrieved the disc of "Red River" from the player, then returned it to its case. "They got a special on hash browns and gravy at the *OK Corral*, unless you wanna go to that new Chinky place on Tenth Street."

"'Chinky' place?" questioned Kris.

"Yeah. The joint's called *Chow Yun No-Fat*. They got the best 'Cream of Sum-Yung Guy' in town!" Marty giggled. "Man, you oughta check out the tight little ass on their cute little waiter! Goddamn, Kris! I wanna whip it out, right here right now, and whack off just thinking of him!"

Kris gritted his teeth in frustration and disgust.

Marty snickered as he cuddled up to Kris. "I love ya, buddy," he said, kissing Kris upon the cheek.

Kris threw his arms around Marty. He fought back the tears seeping from both eyes. He first kissed Marty's forehead, then lips. "Why, Marty?" he breathed. "Why do I love you? And why do you love *me*?"

Marty laughed. "'Cause yer the only dumb sumbitch who can put up with me!"

2

Marty and Kris left the cramped, dirty bedroom, wandered down the cramped, dirty hallway, then entered a cramped, dirty living room and kitchen.

Much of the furniture looked as if it came out of the late-Seventies or early Eighties. Practically everything in the living room had been purchased at the *Goodwill* and *Salvation Army*, or at local flea markets and yard sales.

The couch, which was older than God Himself, missed a leg and was caved in on one side. Potato chips, cookies, and candy wrappers were shoved between or under the cushions, or carelessly tossed behind the couch. Two aging recliners sat in opposite ends of the living room. Every chair was buried under comic books and automotive, gun, or porn magazines. One window was shattered, due to an altercation between Marty and a previous Loser of the Month. Poorly taped and stabled plastic covered the missing window. Damp air and moisture blew in from outside. The room was musty and cold.

Patrick McKenna sat in the middle of a shag carpet on the floor. He played a *Nintendo* game on a twenty-six-inch TV. The television, also an analog, was more than two decades old. In its day, it was a top-of-the-line model. Now, the colors were faded and smudgy.

Patrick was twelve. He resembled Marty, but was shorter. He was soft and plump, not really fat but hardly skinny. He rarely went outdoors, and had the pale complexion to prove it.

Patrick stared at the TV and frantically guided a hero on a long, dangerous quest. His thumbs and fingers hastily worked to operate the video game's controls.

Marty frowned. The last thing he wanted to see was his lard-ass little brother do nothing but lay around on his little lard-ass, until he turned into a gigantic and totally useless lard-ass. "Stupid-ass video games," commented Marty, "for a lazy, good-for-nothin' fat-ass."

Patrick said nothing. He'd heard it all before. Besides, he was too busy concentrating on the game. Excitedly, he fought off monsters with the use of a sword and magic. Outdated sound effects blared from the outdated sound system of the outdated television.

"See that?" groaned Marty. "Retard's head's so full of shit he can't hear a word I say. Just look at 'em, Kris! *Look!* Fatrick can't do nothin' but sit on his fat ass, playing fuckin' video games all day. Too lazy to do a goddamn thing."

"Just like someone else I know," mumbled Kris.

"Them games don't even belong to 'em," added Marty. "They belong to Billy Rodriquez. And if Billy don't get his shit back, he's gonna kick Fatrick's ass till his nose bleeds. Then I'm gonna kick Fatrick's ass till his nose bleeds!"

"*Marty*," scolded Kris.

"Why don'tcha shut your fucking mouth, Marty?" screeched Patrick. "Why can'tcha just leave me alone?"

"You shut your fuckin' mouth, fat-boy!" yelled Marty. He ripped the controls from Patrick's hands, then turned the TV off. "Them ain't even yer fuckin' games! Now pack all this shit up, and haul it back over to Billy's, or throw 'em in the fuckin' garbage for all I care! Just get 'em the fuck outa here!"

Patrick angrily lifted himself from the floor. He clenched his fist and slugged Marty on the chin, as hard as he could.

Seconds later, Marty and Patrick were on the floor, wrestling. Candy wrappers, dishes covered in moldy food, video games, and foul language flew everywhere. Dust and dirt filled the room.

The McKenna brothers' disagreement shook the trailer. A whiskey bottle, sitting on one corner of a bar in the kitchen, hit the tile floor and exploded. Glass shattered in all directions.

Kris stood to one side, watching the contest play out. He'd seen it all before, and already guessed the outcome. Typical early morning at the

McKenna residence.

Marty twisted one of Patrick's arms behind his back, then pressed the younger boy's face into the shag carpet. "Get off o' me!" screamed Patrick. "Get off o' me, or I'll tell Mom!"

"Go ahead, tell Mom!" shouted Marty, his bare knees resting in the center of Patrick's spine. "Go right on ahead and tell Mom! Know what she'll do? Not a goddamn thing! She'll do what she always does... tell me to pack my bags and get the fuck out, before her and Lance run off to get drunk and smoke dope!"

"Marty," bawled Patrick. "Get off o' me, ya fucking faggot!"

"I ain't no fuckin' faggot!" argued Marty.

"Ain't what I heard!" said Patrick. "Everybody knows you and Kris are faggots!"

Kris suddenly felt overwhelmed with panic.

"Everybody knows you guys ass-fuck each other," added Patrick, "then suck your wrinkled, tiny cocks!"

Marty slammed Patrick's head against the floor.

"Keep it down out there!" hollered Lance, from the master bedroom. "Or I'm coming in there to ya!"

"Faggot!" cried Patrick, tears spilling from his eyes. "Faggot, faggot, faggot... *Faggot!* Fudge-packing, cocksucking faggot! You and Kris are cocksucking, fudge-packing faggots!"

"I don't give a fuck what yer lazy-ass says about us," said Marty, slowly getting off of Patrick as he wiped dust from his hoody, cutoffs, and legs. "Keep yer fuckin' mouth shut about me and Kris. Ya got that?"

Patrick painfully sat up, wiping his dampened nose and eyes while agonizing from the punishment which Marty meted him.

"Ya got that?" repeated Marty. "Keep yer fuckin' mouth shut about me and Kris!"

"I heard," moped Patrick.

"You get all this shit packed up and haul it back to Billy's," ordered Marty. "Or I'm gonna. Then I'm gonna kick yer ass from here to fuckin' Portland!"

Grudgingly, Patrick did as he was told. He began collecting Billy's games and console then threw them into a nearby cardboard box, all the while mumbling profanities under his breath.

"Buy ya breakfast at the *OK Corral*," Marty told Kris, as if nothing ever happened. "Whadda ya say, buddy? How 'bout it?"

3

Marty and Kris went outside to a wet, dreary day. Despite the crummy weather, it still beat the heated climate within the *Fleetwood* trailer.

The two teens walked along a one-way lane, separating dozens of mobile homes. There was little activity.

One judged those residing in each trailer, based on the music which played inside them. An older couple listened to classic Country and Western, generally George Jones, Patsy Cline, and Roy Acuff. A nearby couple went for the more contemporary style of Alan Jackson and Kenny Chesney. Meanwhile, a middle-aged widower liked Bach, Beethoven, and Mozart.

Patrick's remarks about 'faggots' upset Kris. There was little truth about the insults, at least the 'fudge-packing' and 'cocksucking' bit.

Not yet, anyway.

Kris gulped once he realized that his love for Marty McKenna was an open secret. He wished no one knew about it. Seemingly, *everyone* in town knew.

"Gee, Marty," said Kris, hoping to change the subject. "You guys ever think about cleaning your house?"

"Gee, Kris," responded Marty. "Ever think about mindin' yer own fuckin' business?"

"Just saying, Marty...."

"Don't bother sayin' it at all!"

Kris shrugged. "Never mind."

Marty lived off the beaten path, away from the hustle and bustle from Grangeford's busier streets and thoroughfares. His was a neighborhood of eroding pavement, gravel roads, decaying homes and buildings, low income, neglect and despair. The community wasn't spared the economic ravages of a severe economic downturn. Few areas weren't without at least one FOR SALE sign.

In the past, timber, agriculture, and mining subsidized Grangeford. Now the city struggled to reinvent itself. Mills closed, as their wages with benefits and perks disappeared. Many folks sought greener pastures elsewhere. Others chose to remain and settle for lesser money, with little or nothing set aside for a rainy day.

Even the commercial districts of town felt the pinch. Mom and pop stores, which once characterized Grangeford for decades, folded up and faded away. Their picturesque storefronts fell into disrepair... painful reminders of what used to be or what might have been. Businesses moved from Main Street and relocated near the interstate freeway. Fields, which used to raise cattle and alfalfa, became home to shopping malls and chain stores.

Marty and Kris walked at a slow, meandering pace. It was Sunday, in early-June. There was little traffic, and most businesses didn't open until eleven on the Sabbath, if they even bothered opening at all. The downtown was empty, as many people went to church or slept in.

The teens wandered along backstreets and alleys, surrounded by crumbling brick and mortar monoliths, some ten-stories tall. The narrow lanes were laced with garbage, graffiti, and debris. Empty basements and buildings were hideaways for drug and alcohol abuse, or used for sexual journeys, adventures, and escapades. It was among these corridors where Marty and Kris encountered two of their least favorite schoolmates. The Dirtbag, real name Mike Moyers, and his one and only friend, Turtlehead, real name Corey Phipps.

Mike was the Dirtbag because he changed his clothes an average of once every six years, and had the foul stench to prove it. His plaid, woolen jacket was dusty, dirty, and threadbare. His jeans and shoes were filled with holes. His few teeth were black, rotten, and missing. Even his gross red pimples had gross red pimples. His shaggy, uncombed hair and ugly attempts to grow facial hair were havens for germs and insects.

Turtlehead was Turtlehead because his head looked like it belonged to a turtle. His lack of smarts and perpetual moronic expressions reenforced the crude nickname. His endless, dorky stares, Coke-bottle eyeglasses, and drooling mouth stated that no thoughts dared enter his thick skull, in fear of being lost forever.

Marty frowned as he approached the Dirtbag and Turtlehead. He regretted going down that particular alleyway. Only stoners, druggies, and gutter trash hung out there. Marty already knew he was trailer-trash, all right, yet had more class in his little finger than the Dirtbag and Turtlehead combined. He tried to ignore the two lowlifes, in hopes they'd go away.

"If you two homos are looking for somewhere to screw, you came to the wrong place," said the Dirtbag, wearing that same shit-eating grin he always wore prior to getting his ass beat, which he was about to do.

"You mean to say that you two homos beat us to it?" answered Marty. "Hell, I never thought Turtlehead was one to put out. I never thought that imbecile was one to put out. Jesus! He's so fuckin' ugly, even his right hand won't put out."

"Want me to crush your fucking skull in?" threatened the Dirtbag, his shit-eating grin altering to a shit-eating frown. His breath came off as an odor, suggesting he'd been hitting the haybale cigarettes and airplane glue a lot lately. "If I had my way, we'd wipe all queers out, the same way Hitler wiped out the Kikes in World War I."

"World War II, dickhead," commented Marty. "And if you wanna wipe all the queers out, why don'tcha start with me and Kris?"

"Marty," warned Kris. "Let's get out of here...."

"Your butt-buddy's right," said the Dirtbag, struggling to control his temper. "Get lost, before I mop the floor with your scrawny ass..."

"'Floor'?" laughed Marty. "Shit, man! This is an alley, not a floor. But hey.... No fault of yer own. You and yer fuckin' family's so fuckin' stupid you can't even tell the difference."

The Dirtbag's eyes bugged out.

"So," taunted Marty, "what motivated yer old man to move the family to the city landfill? That the only place in town they can't evict ya?"

"Shut the fuck up about my family, *McKenna!*" the Dirtbag shrieked. He said 'McKenna' as if it was, in of itself, an insult.

"Then shut the fuck up about Kris and me!" ordered Marty.

"Marty...." repeated Kris, anxiously.

"At least I wasn't conceived in the men's room of some backwater greasy spoon," said the Dirtbag. "Not like the rest of you crack babies."

Marty backhanded the Dirtbag's face.

Initially, the Dirtbag didn't know who or what had struck him, until he noticed Marty's wild-eyed grin. Kris backed away, while Turtlehead stood to one side, wearing a dumb, blank expression.

"Just wanted to see how easy it was to bitch-slap a worthless piece of shit like you," said Marty, smugly. "Too easy, man... way too fuckin' easy!"

The Dirtbag said nothing. He wanted to say plenty. None of it was proper or polite. He didn't think Marty was capable of laying a hand on him.

The alley grew deathly quiet.

"Hey guys," said Kris, diplomatically stepping between Marty and the Dirtbag. "This is getting nowhere. C'mon, Marty. Let's get out of here...."

The Dirtbag shoved Kris out of his way, then attacked Marty.

Kris staggered backwards, and nearly fell over a steel garbage can which lay on its side due to the breeze. The Dirtbag sent a fist straight into Marty's nose.

"Fuckin' pussy!" giggled Marty, blinking once or twice but hardly phased. "Y' hit like a fuckin' pussy!"

Once more, the Dirtbag made contact with Marty, this time in the ribs. Marty responded by landing a left undercut to the Dirtbag's chin. The Dirtbag toppled over like a domino, into an oily mudpuddle.

"You want some of it?" Marty asked Turtlehead, trying to sound like John Wayne in "Red River".

Startled by what had just happened to the Dirtbag, Turtlehead shook his head, 'no'.

The Dirtbag attempted to get back on his wobbly feet. No good. Unable to stand, he remained on his backside, soaking wet from the dampened concrete. "Gonna kick your sorry ass, McKenna!" he screamed, his shrill voice echoing through the alley. "Gonna stomp shit outa you and your bed-buddy!"

"That'll be the day," said Marty, inciting a noted line from *The Searchers*. He turned toward Kris. "Come on, Blankethead."

Kris shrugged, took a deep breath, and sighed.

Marty never ceased to amaze him. He grudgingly admired Marty's ability to take a wallop. At the same time, Kris feared that eventually Marty would meet his match suffer defeat. He didn't know whether to lament or look forward to that day.

Kris shot a quick glance at the Dirtbag, then toward Turtlehead, before following Marty onto the *OK Corral.*

4

"*Guide me, O thou great redeemer,*" sang Marty, as he and Kris neared the OK Corral, on Main Street. "*Pilgrim through this barren land; I am weak, but thou art mighty, Hold me with thy powerful hand...*

"*Bread of heaven, Bread of heaven! Feed me till I need no more... Need no more! Feed me till I need no more!*"

Kris frowned. He wouldn't have minded Marty's singing so much... had Marty been a decent singer. One imagined that Marty wished to sing in the worst way. In an odd sort of way, he succeeded.

He sang in the *worst* way.

Marty knowingly drew attention to himself. He lacked a thought or care in the world, as if to tell everyone to go screw themselves. My name's Marty McKenna, and if ya don't like it then look the other way...

... and while you're at it, get the hell outa my way!

On the other hand, Kris wanted to be invisible, unrecognizable, anonymous. He simply wished to enter the restaurant, have a quick breakfast, and get on with his day. That wasn't so much to ask for, was it? It was never easy to quietly get through life when Marty was around. Marty sought to be the center of attention and, regrettably, Kris was forced to go along with the ride.

Yet, even if Marty habitually drove him crazy, Kris still loved him. He just couldn't help it! He loved Marty for a number of reasons. One, Marty was Kris' friend, when Kris feared he had no friends.

Two, Kris was in love with Marty. Marty was his boyfriend, the one he wished to spend the rest of his life with.

Finally, he loved Marty simply for being Marty, even if being Marty meant being so unpredictable, rude, and obnoxious.

Kris and Marty were an *item*.

Kris would've preferred had most people not known it. Yes, he loved Marty, wanted to love Marty, and sought Marty's love and approval. He only begged to love Marty quietly, where only a select few were aware of their relationship.

And yet, there was the bizarre sight of two gay teens, going to breakfast one rainy Sunday. Instead of being a couple of regular guys, one kid sought to draw attention to himself by singing an old Welsh hymn while showing off his legs in short-shorts... and enjoying every minute of it!

There were few pedestrians on Main Street that morning. Try as they may, folks were unable to ignore Marty's singing. Kris dreaded what they may have thought as they stared at Marty, like he was a sideshow freak.

Faggots. That's likely what everyone thought of Kris and Marty. *Faggots.* Why don't those two faggots keep it to themselves, or (better yet!) simply drop dead? Or, better yet, why don't they do the world a big favor by killing themselves? Get them outa our miseries, by killing themselves?

"C'mon, Kris, sing!" cheered Marty. "Sing with me, buddy!"

"I accidentally forgot the words," said Kris.

"Accidentally forgot the words?"

"Yeah," responded Kris. "Accidentally on purpose."

"I swear, Kristoffer, you ain't no fun at all!"

"Who said you were?"

"I'm always fun!" laughed Marty.

"You wish," breathed Kris, tiredly.

"I know," said Marty, as he and Kris entered a small restaurant and tavern known as the *OK Corral*. Country music played from a tinny jukebox in the tavern. Reproductions of Frederic Remington and Charlie Russell paintings decorated the walls, along with black and white photographs of Grangeford in days long past. Antlers, a cougar hide, and other trophies were displayed throughout the establishment.

Sounds of pool balls smacking together could be heard from the tavern, as men cheered and jeered at their success or failure at billiards. A few town drunks and old-timers bellied up to the bar.

The inviting smell of bacon, sausage, potatoes and eggs greeted Kris and Marty, along with the warmth, comfort, and assurance of familiar surroundings.

"Of all the gin joints in all the towns in all the world," commented Marty, leading Kris to a darkened booth, "I gotta eat in this scroungy shit-hole of a dive..."

Kris bit his bottom lip and prayed no one else heard what Marty had just said.

Two servers, a younger guy and an older woman, rushed around the diner as they fulfilled breakfast orders. Bonita had worked at the OK Corral for more than thirty years, and showed no signs of slowing down. Her gray hair, baggy eyes, and wrinkled brow failed to reveal the energy and enthusiasm she held toward her regular customers.

The younger server was Mark McKenna, Marty's twenty-one-year-old brother.

Mark was handsome and, like Marty, short-in-stature. He kept his fiery red hair trimmed neatly. Although he had shaved that morning, spots of whiskers already dotted his face.

Where Marty was thin and lean, Mark was muscular and stocky. In high school, Mark played on the defensive line for the Grangeford Bobcats. Some claimed he was the defensive line. Mark rated highest in the number of tackles for the league, as well as the top five for the entire state. He earned a B-average in school, was a member of the Letterman's Club, and editor of the student newspaper, the *Bobcat Weekly*.

Mark never applied for grants, loans, or scholarship for higher education. He began working at the *OK Corral* when he was fifteen. Six years later, he remained there.

As well, Mark still lived at home with his mom, two younger siblings, and the current Loser of the Month. It wasn't a question of choice, but rather obligation. It had nothing to do with supporting his mother or Lance Copperfield. Mark loved Patrick and Marty dearly, and paid the bills to compensate for his mom's deficiencies and failings. Mark gained little praise, gratitude, or recognition from his mom or the Loser of the Month.

The passing of time had not been kind to Mark McKenna. He was employed, all right, yet his wheels were spinning. His old chums were no longer in Grangeford. They enrolled in college, went into the military, or held jobs in cities as Portland, Eugene, Astoria, Salem, Spokane, the Tri-Cities, Bend or Boise. Most were married, happy, and content.

Meanwhile, Mark was still in Grangeford.

Mark still lived at home.

Mark still worked at the *OK Corral.*

Mark spent long, sleepless nights wishing for something else.... Something better. He was dating Kris' older sister Jennifer, and their relationship had gotten serious. Jennifer also worked at the *OK Corral*, as a bartender. Neither were satisfied, and often discussed an exit strategy out of Grangeford. Both had their sights on either attending *Oregon State* or the *University of Oregon*. Mark hoped to study creative writing, while Jennifer aimed on a degree in art.

Both Mark and Jennifer were committed to their younger siblings. Such commitments endangered their own ambitions and prospects.

Mark and Jennifer were aware of Kris and Marty's relationship, and remained protective and supportive. They even considered including adding Kris, Marty, and Patrick in on their escape from Grangeford, to a community where they'd be more accepted. This arrangement wouldn't be without costs. Everyone had to carry their own weight. This was difficult, since Kris, Marty, and Patrick were minors, and in school. Mark and Jennifer didn't wish to leave their younger siblings behind. Regrettably, both grew increasingly more tired and dreary of their dead-end existences.

Mark approached Kris and Marty.

The McKenna brothers began to snicker, as if they held onto mutual secrets, never to be discussed with others. A blind man could see that Mark and Marty loved each other, had their backs, and were willing to live or die together, as only brothers could.

Kris felt safe with Mark McKenna. He had nothing to hide nor conceal around him. Nor did he have to explain or apologize for the way he was. He wasn't threatened, endangered, or made to feel inferior in Mark's company.

Marty was Kris' first and only love. Kris realized from the sixth grade that he was different, which separated him from many of his male classmates. At first, he responded with denial, and the shedding of tears. Self-loathing and resentment soon followed. Kris didn't want to be gay, and was terrified. He couldn't flee from his attraction to certain guys. Kris avoided gym classes, so he'd never have to shower with objects of his affection.

Thoughts of his homosexuality tore at Kris, to the point where he contemplated jumping into the Grande Ronde River. In time, his decaying body would eventually be recovered from large stones or a log jam.

Marty never held back nor denied his sexuality. Publicly, he revealed no shame, no pity, no self-hatred toward himself. At the same time, he wasn't one to flaunt it by attending rallies, carry rainbow flags, or participate in pride parades. He wished to co-exist in the "straight" world, providing it didn't deliberately get in the way or step on his toes.

Kris and Marty first met in the third grade at North Grangeford Elementary. Neither imagined that the other kid was destined to be "that way". Years later, when Kris finally broke down and made tearful confessions, did Marty voice similar revelations. In Marty's case, his coming out was laced with self-deprecating humor and maniacal laughter, worthy of Walter Huston's performance at the end of *The Treasure of the Sierra Madre*. Initially, Kris and Marty joined forces out of unity, safety, trust and confidence. Mutual attraction blossomed into romance and dating.

Everyone knew Marty McKenna was gay. He never claimed otherwise. He rarely avoided confrontation or a knock-down, drag-out brawl, when it came to upholding himself or others like him. Marty wasn't afraid of anything! Or was he? Was Marty's brazen actions, profane language, and Devil-May-Care attitude a façade to bury unspeakable pain and trauma?

"So, how's Peckinpah today?" Marty asked Mark.

"Mean and bloody as hell." Mark grinned.

Marty jokingly insisted that Mark write a series of Adult Westerns involving a blood-soaked, thunder-driven anti-hero named Peckinpah Ford Leone, who took part in grisly shoot-outs when he wasn't banging every prostitute around. It was a running gag which Mark and Marty spent long hours discussing.

"Has he killed Jack Palance and Jack Elam yet?" asked Marty.

"No," answered Mark. "He barely got around to blasting Albert Salmi, Albert Dekker, and Albert E. Newman,"

"You mean he hasn't shot Bruce Dern and Bruce Cabot yet?"

"Naw. He has yet to hang Lee Marvin and Lee Van Cleef." Mark cleared his throat. "What will it be today, gentlemen?"

Kris and Marty ordered Cokes and sausage breakfast sandwiches.

Mark scribbled the order down then ran it to Luis, the day cook.

"Man, look at the tight little ass on that rootin-tootin' cowpoke," whispered Marty, motioning toward a young ranch hand who had just entered the diner for a cup of joe. "Beats watching Brokeback Mountain any day!"

Kris sighed.

"What?" laughed Marty.

"Why, Marty?" Kris shrugged. "Why do you always say that stuff?"

"What stuff, Kris?"

"'Look at the tight little ass on that rootin' tootin' cowpoke'," mumbled Kris. "Why can't we just have a normal conversation without it getting... so dirty?"

"Just making an observation," said Marty. "Just wanted ya to have a peek at that guy's sweet little bottom, that's all. Makes ya wonder what he's got in the front. A thousand-and-one wet dreams, if y'ask me."

"Marty!"

Marty giggled.

Kris bit his bottom lip. He was torn between cupping Marty's hand in his, or storming out of the OK Corral, and Marty McKenna's life, forever. Still, he couldn't deny his love for Marty, and didn't wish to part with him, not for a single, solitary moment! Even then, he got tired of Marty's anger, potty mouth, and fighting.

In a way, Kris owed Marty a great deal, including levels of happiness and peace of mind. However, at what point would he grow weary of Marty's volatile behavior, and seek a more sane, stable, and caring relationship?

"I love you," whispered Marty, gazing into Kris' watery eyes. "Love ya, man."

"I love you, too," answered Kris.

Marty chuckled. "Look, I dunno why ya get so worked up all the time. Everyone knows I'm just jokin'."

"It's not joking to me!" snapped Kris.

Kris and Marty stared at each other for several seconds. "Aw, what the hell, Kris?" Marty mumbled, finally. "Just forget about...."

"What about that crap of you dropping your pants before I got to your room, earlier?" questioned Kris.

"What of it?"

"Did you really expect me to?" Kris sighed. "Did you really expect me to have sex with you, right then and there, with your mom and Lance in the next room?"

"Well, hell." Marty frowned. "If I knew ya felt that way about it."

Kris gritted his teeth. He had already made out with Marty, months before, in the confines of a tent during an overnight outing on a camping trip in the Elkhorn Mountains. That's as far as it went. Was Marty's taunt yet another prank, or an invitation to get down-and-dirty in that filthy, disgusting bedroom?

"So, do you wanna do it?" asked Marty, in a serious tone. "Do you wanna do it with me, Kris? Do ya?"

Kris was uncertain. Yes, he loved Marty, more than anything! He often fantasized about making love with Marty. Was he ready to take their relationship that much further? Or was Marty ready, for that matter?

"It depends, Marty," said Kris, bluntly. "Do *you*?"

5

Kris and Marty sipped their Cokes and awaited their breakfast sandwiches.

Both had posed the same question to their companion... that of the physical act of lovemaking. Both left the question unanswered. It didn't prevent them from mulling over it, or to even contemplate such possibilities.

Yeah, Kris did love Marty. And yeah, he did fantasize about making love to him. Yet, Kris was at odds, regarding a strong Christian upbringing which stated that homosexuality was an abomination. Did God hate gay people? And, as a result, did He hate Kris and Marty? Or was it just those who claimed to worship God who hated Kris and Marty?

Kris never asked to be gay. Sometimes he never wanted it. Certain folks argued that he and Marty were in league with Satan...an unspeakable thought!

Kris still loved God. He sure didn't love Satan! He wished to be loved by those who worshipped and feared God. He also wanted to be an upstanding, respected member of a church family.

Kris also sought love and approval by his parents...the same parents who ordered him out of the house last February, during a cold, blustery snowstorm.

Thank God for 'Crazy' Aunt Barbara, the family oddball, the outcast, the black sheep. The family member no one was supposed to mention in good company.

Thank God for 'Crazy' Aunt Barbara, who never thought twice about offering Kris her old sewing room for as long as he needed it. Thank God for 'Crazy' Aunt Barbara, who housed Kris, supported him, accepted him, loved him, and never spoke unfavorably for who he was or what he was.

Aunt Barbara was in her early-sixties, and spent much of her youth engaged in activities frowned upon by others. She left home at age fifteen, moved in with guys wearing hair longer than hers, and occupied houses with no phone, no electricity, no indoor plumbing. Occasionally, she even lived in cars. Twice, she hitchhiked from one end of the United States to the other.

In her younger, wilder, stupider days, Barbara smoked every sort of weed imaginable, and went on trips without leaving the house. She married the wrong men, got her head caved in and her teeth knocked out by those she misjudged and misunderstood, and somehow lived to talk about it. She now laughed at her own misdeeds, misconceptions, and misadventures.

Barbara eventually became a social worker, and spoke against her former lifestyle without ever denying it. She mentored and tutored kids from the tough side of the tracks, and helped guide them to happiness and stability.

Barbara upheld Kris and Marty, simply for being Kris and Marty. She didn't care if they were in love. She openly encouraged their relationship. She even pushed them to express their love fully (*with protection, of course!*).

Aunt Barbara was an unhindered, free spirit. She argued that Kris had to live life on life's terms, by taking risks and taking chances. And if taking risks and taking chances meant loving Marty McKenna, then so be it.

With that in mind, would Kris give himself permission to love Marty McKenna?

6

Kris and Marty enjoyed their breakfast when they got a surprise visit from Patrick and his twelve-year-old pal, Billy Rodriquez.

Once he and Billy entered the OK Corral, Patrick let out a high-pitched shriek like he was dying. This caught the attention of everyone inside the diner. Patrick had a bruised cheek, a knot on his forehead, and a black eye.

Billy was a short, dark-skinned boy. He wore a black, turtleneck sweater, a few sizes too large, baggy plaid shorts, and untied sneakers. His hair was thick and unruly. Although he didn't make a sound as he got inside, Billy still looked angry and upset.

"What the motherfuck?" grunted Marty, glaring at Patrick. "Fuck's yer problem? Eat all the goddamn Twinkies, and now you expect me to buy ya more?"

"Dirt.... Dirt.... Dirt...." stuttered Patrick, wiping his teary eyes as he fought to get the words out.

"The fuck're you moanin' about?" demanded Marty, both frustrated and worried.

"Pat was taking my games back over to my place," explained Billy, "when he got stopped by Turtlehead and the Dirtbag."

Kris and Marty's eyes widened.

"They beat Pat all up!" shouted Billy. "Then took my games!"

"Motherfuckin', cocksuckin' sons o' bitches!" cursed Marty, loud enough for all to hear. "Where are them two piles of shit? Where the fuck are they? I wanna beat the livin' shit outa..."

"Wait!" called Kris, stopping Marty as he stormed toward the door. "Find out what happened first, before we..."

"I a'ready know what the fuck happened!" yelled Marty. "I know enough a'ready to go beat the shit outa' them two assholes!"

"Marty," urged Kris. "Maybe we should contact the police."

"We don't need the police," stated Marty. "I'm gonna handle this myself. I don't wanna get the fuckin' cops involved."

Mark, Bonita, and Luis stepped from the kitchen to check on Patrick and Billy. Luis was a large, burly man with coal-black hair, graying at the sideburns, and a receding mustache. Bonita fetched a box of *Kleenex* to remove the blood from Patrick's face. Mark sat Patrick at Kris and Marty's table. Meanwhile, Luis fixed a couple of milkshakes for Patrick and Billy, on the house.

"I.... I was just taking Billy's games back," sobbed Patrick, ashamed and embarrassed because everyone in the diner stared at him.

"And then what?" asked Mark. "Please tell me, Pat. Then what? What did Mike and Corey do to you?"

As he slurped his milkshake down, Patrick said that he had met the Dirtbag and Turtlehead somewhere on the railroad tracks, not far from Monroe Avenue. The Dirtbag wished to take his anger out on someone for what Marty had done to him earlier... and that someone was Patrick McKenna.

The Dirtbag snatched the games away from Patrick, then proceeded to beat on him. Despite Patrick's pleas to stop, the Dirtbag never held back in torturing him. He got Patrick down on the wet ground, then laughingly slugged his face, crotch, and gut. Later, he shoved dirt, mud, and gravel into Patrick's shirt and pants.

Turtlehead didn't lay a finger on Patrick. At the same time, he did nothing to stop the Dirtbag from injuring the youngster. He simply stood to one side and watched it happen.

"We better call the cops," suggested Bonita. Several customers agreed with her.

"To hell with the cops," said Luis. "Time to kick those little bastards square in their asses, then shoot their parents for not raising them right."

"Fuckin' A!" cheered Marty, spurred on by Luis' rant.

"And I think we ought to contact their folks," said Kris. "Let them handle it."

"And I think we oughta kill them two assholes!" snapped Marty. "Kill both them sons o' bitches, then leave their rotten corpses on their family's front porch to stink things up."

"I only want my games back," said Billy, vacantly.

Mark was plagued with uncertainty. He was an adult now, and had to handle things as such. He was no fan of Mike Moyers, and wanted to see the bully punished for what he did to Patrick. However, he couldn't approve of Marty's actions against Mike, earlier. As a result, Mark believed much of the blame had to be pinned on Marty.

It was maddening! Mark loved Marty. There was nothing he wouldn't do for his younger brothers. Yet, hardly a week went by where Marty got into fights with punks, troublemakers, or the current Loser of the Month. Mark wondered if Marty's tendencies to fisticuffs were a means of defending his sexuality, or as a rebellion against the harsh realities of life.

Maybe Marty simply enjoyed brawling. He had never lost a single fight in his entire life. That crazy, unpredictable little Scots-Irish American was as tough as leather, as stubborn as a mule, and dumber than a post.

"Don't start anything, Marty," begged Mark. "We got enough troubles as it is, with Mom constantly using the money I give her to blow in bars, or at the liquor store."

"I never start nothin'," said Marty. "I only finish it."

"Damn it, Marty!" cursed Mark. "Whatcha gonna do if the cops get involved, and you end up taking the rap?"

"What happens if the Dirtbag gets away for what he done to Fatrick," argued Marty, "and we all come off lookin' like pussies?"

"I don't have the time, money, or inkling to bail you out," said Mark. "You know how it is. Instead of nailing Mike Moyers, they'll hang you instead. We don't need that, Marty."

Marty glared at Mark, in contempt.

"You want to kick hell out of everyone," said Mark. "One of these days, bud, the world's gonna kick back."

Marty only chuckled.

Mark took a deep breath, then released it in a sigh. He gave Marty an expression of love, mixed with defeat and grudging resignation. He slowly returned to his duties as a server.

Kris knew something had to be done to recover Billy's games, and for what happened to Patrick. He wondered, yet doubted, if the Dirtbag would return the games without a fuss.

The Dirtbag wasn't smart, nor did he toe the line. Like most of his siblings, he was a known thief. The Grangeford police and county mounties constantly paid the Moyers a visit, to retrieve stolen property. Mike was often responsible for many of the disruptions at school. He sassed teachers and administrators, had the lousiest grades, despised authority, held no prospects and likely no future. Likely, he'd end up in prison.

The only member of that clan who stood a chance was Lester. He distanced himself from the others, and forged a positive name and reputation in the community. Lester enlisted in the Army, spent a year or so in the Middle East, then settled into civilian life with a wife, two kids, a decent job, a Toyota Tacoma, and a hunting dog.

Kris contemplated his own life. Thank God for Crazy Aunt Barbara, who offered him a place to stay after he got kicked out of the house. Barbara's generosity prevented Kris from throwing himself into the river, which was his first inclination.

Then there was Marty McKenna...

Kris loved Marty. This truth gave him some level of happiness, along with drama and despair. Loving Marty definitely had its share of joy and unpredictability. Marty was never boring. He was always interesting, if not downright scandalous.

Kris stepped outside to a damp, dreary, drizzly morning. The cloud cover had thickened, with scant promise of sunlight. The traffic on Main Street had gradually picked up, though not as hectic as on weekdays. Many churches had completed their Sunday services. People went home, or had brunch at local diners. A couple of teen boys, both members of the LDS, zipped by on ten-speed bicycles. They were both bright-eyed, seemingly innocent, and clean. They were dressed in dark slacks, spit-shined shoes, white shirts and ties. They smiled at Kris as they passed by, laughing amongst themselves. The blinking neon sign of a competing tavern across the street caught Kris' attention, through the haze and low-hanging fog.

Kris stood under the restaurant eve, staying dry but hardly warm. A cool breeze swept through the concrete and steel canyon of Main Street. Kris glanced at his bare, pale legs, wishing he hadn't worn shorts in such crummy weather.

Jennifer English was a bartender at the *OK Corral*. She was Kris' older sister, and had a maternal nature toward her younger siblings. She had just turned twenty-one, and had just gotten her license to serve booze from the *Oregon Liquor Control Commission*, after months of washing dishes and waiting tables. She had the same hair color, round face, and fair complexion as Kris.

Jennifer excused herself from the bar, then went outside for a smoke. She also wished to chat with Kris. Eagerly, she threw her arms around Kris and embraced him. "Morning, Little Brother," she greeted.

"Morning, Big Sister," said Kris, unable to hide the anxiety in his voice.

"So, how's Crazy Aunt Barbara?"

"Crazy as usual. She spent the morning telling me stories about her adventures with oatmeal and marijuana cookies."

"What's troubling you, Little Brother?" said Jennifer. She always referred to Kris as 'Little Brother', although he was more than a foot taller. "No need to keep secrets from me. I'll get to the truth, sooner or later. Might as well tell me now, and save me the grief."

"It's...Marty," said Kris, evasively.

"*Marty?*"

Kris smiled at his own expense. "Yeah...Marty."

"It's always about Marty," commented Jennifer. "Never about you."

Kris shrugged, as if to ask 'What can I say?'

Jennifer motioned toward a small, wooden bench in front of the diner. "Sit down, Little Brother. There's something we need to talk about."

Kris did as he was told.

"Kris," said Jennifer, resting one hand on her brother's knee. "Mark and I have been talking. We're thinking strongly of moving somewhere to the Willamette Valley, maybe Eugene or Corvallis. Next spring, at the very latest."

Kris' heart skipped a beat. Similar to Aunt Barbara, Jennifer was one of the few members of the family who never condemned him for his sexuality. Kris felt threatened and endangered by prospects of Mark and Jennifer's departure. They had long discussed possibilities of leaving Grangeford to pursue higher education, careers, getting married, and having children.

"This town's killing Mark!" explained Jennifer. "He hates working here, and keeps threatening to quit one of these days. Not only does he no longer want to wait tables, he wants out of that disgusting trailer. If it wasn't for Pat and Marty, he would've left months ago."

Kris felt the earth sweep out from under him.

"We hope to take you with us," said Jennifer. "If we can...If you can...

If you're able."

"If you leave, I leave!" asserted Kris. "Crazy Aunt Barbara's one thing. I can't make it without you, Big Sister!"

Mark wants Marty and Pat to come with us, but..." Jennifer stopped. "But...but what?"

"It's wonderful that you and Marty are together, and that you found each other. But, well..." Jennifer sighed. "Marty's Marty. Guess he just can't help himself."

Kris smiled, warily. "Yeah. Marty's Marty."

"There's nothing I wouldn't do for Marty," said Jennifer. "Mark keeps talking about taking him with us, but... I just wonder if Marty's smart enough, wise enough, and mature enough."

Kris was blinded by his devotion to Marty. Had he given himself time to think about it, he pondered if he truly loved Marty, or was merely in love with him. He was too close to the situation, and felt trapped by it.

"I hope it works out between you and Marty," said Jennifer, doubtfully. "Really, I can't help but to like Marty, but... Marty's Marty. He simply can't help himself. What can I say? Marty's Marty."

"Yeah," mumbled Kris. "Marty's Marty."

"I have to get back to work." said Jennifer patted Kris' leg as she stood. "I hope it works out between you and Marty, and that he can come with us. But if it doesn't, there's other fish in the sea."

Kris lowered his head.

"Trust me, Kris," assured Jennifer. "There's always other fish in the sea. If Marty won't take the time to tell you just how special you really are, then some other guy will."

"Thanks," said Kris, his throat tightening.

Jennifer gave Kris a kiss on the cheek. "I love you, Little Brother. You're the best there's ever been!"

Kris was deeply touched and flattered.

Jennifer smiled. "Anyway, I just decided. You're coming with us! You're too awesome to wither away and die in this crappy little Podunk!"

"Thanks," said Kris, so happy he nearly cried.

"Do what it takes to come with us." Once again, Jennifer kissed Kris. "I just don't think you can make it without us, or if I can make if without you. I'll always be there for you, no matter what. I'm always there for you!"

7

"Hey, Kris...Remember that night we fucked next to the boneyard flagpole?"

Kris and Marty had left the *OK Corral*, then went out looking for the Dirtbag and Turtlehead, to retrieve Billy Rodriquez' games and get even for Patrick's beating.

The darkened clouds overhead slowly dissipated. Hazy, blue skies revealed themselves in the east and north. Bright streaks of sunlight illuminated the majestic grandeur and towering peaks of the Wallowa Mountains.

It was mid-June. The mountaintops were still layered in thin snow. Rain and drizzle were replaced by a cold, brisk wind. The forecast called for scattered showers in the evening, then clear skies in the early morning. It made for a good argument to cover flower plants and gardens with coffee cans or sheets of plastic, in case of frost.

Marty and Kris left the major thoroughfares of Grangeford, to the more desolate, slummier, crummier, and scummier neighborhoods. It was even slummier, crummier, and scummier than Marty's part of town. Ornery, unleashed dogs barked and howled from behind fences. Stray, feral cats scurried across single-lane, dirt and gravel lanes. The faint smell of a skunk blew in from somewhere.

Kris and Marty weren't alone. They were joined by Patrick and Billy, who tagged along to fetch the games as well as watch the Dirtbag and Turtlehead get a trouncing.

Kris and Marty preferred not having the younger boys with them. Billy wasn't so much of a problem. He was so quiet that his presence was hardly felt. However, Patrick griped endlessly on the distance he was forced to walk. He was in lousy shape, and constantly begged to stop for a rest.

As the four lads strolled by the Grangeford Cemetery, Marty asked, "Hey, Kris.... Remember that night we fucked next to the boneyard flagpole?"

Kris' mouth dropped open. His complexion turned ashen and pale. Knowing that Marty asked such a question with such honesty and sincerity gave it undue and undeserved credibility. Had Marty made that foolish inquiry when he and Kris were alone, it wouldn't have been a big deal. Regrettably, Patrick and Billy also heard it, which made it more offensive, embarrassing, and insulting.

It didn't help when Patrick looked Kris straight in the eye and laughed. Kris' heart race. Sweat streamed from his face and forehead.

"I know you guys kinda like each other," spoke Billy, in a 'who cares' manner. "Pat a'ready told me you guys are gay. No big deal to me."

Kris glared at Patrick. Whether he 'liked' Marty or not, the whole world didn't have to know about it! "We never fucked next to the flagpole!" Kris scolded Marty. "Or ... or anywhere else for that matter! You and I never fucked at all, Marty!"

"Do ya wanna?" asked Marty. "Later tonight, when it's dark and quiet and we're all by our lonesome?"

"At the rate we're going," sighed Kris, "you and I are never gonna fuck at all."

Patrick snickered, while Billy seemed oblivious to it all.

"Aw, ya know me better'n that," said Marty, casually lighting a cigarette and taking a puff. "You oughta know by now that I'm just jokin'."

"Are you, Marty?" demanded Kris.

"Get over it, Kristoffer!" shouted Marty. "Just get over it, will ya? Only reason I say that shit is to deal with boredom."

"'Boredom'?" gasped Kris.

"Yeah," said Marty. "I don't want ya to think I'm ignorin' ya."

Kris shook his head and sighed.

Marty grinned. "I was afraid you might think I didn't love ya anymore."

"Next time, please ignore me," begged Kris. "If I ever get so bored as to put up with your idiotic questions, just shoot me."

"Don't talk like that," said Marty. "Why, if someone shot ya, who'd put up with my dirty jokes, or take care o' me in my old age?"

"Faggots," mumbled Patrick.

Marty slapped Patrick across the back of his head.

"Hey!" screamed Patrick. "Why'd you do that, for?"

"Might be that I'm a faggot," growled Marty. "Might be that Kris and me are both faggots..."

Kris frowned.

"Least I ain't a lazy, fat little fuck like you," said Marty. "You keep yer fuckin' mouth shut about Kris and me, or I'll report yer worthless, lazy ass to the *NAACP!*"

Patrick laughed. "*NAACP*? You ain't no nigger!"

"Just gettin' around to noticin' that, fat boy?"

"It ain't my fault I'm fat," whined Patrick. "The doctor said it was on account of my genes."

"Yer jeans?" argued Marty. "Only problem with yer jeans is that yer too fuckin' fat to squeeze into 'em!"

"It ain't my fault for being fat," said Patrick. "But it sure the fuck's your fault for being a faggot!"

"That ain't my fault! The school shrink said I was born that way!"

"The fuck you was!"

"The fuck I wasn't!"

"It's your fault for being totally fucked in the head, Marty!" cackled Patrick. "It ain't normal for guys to get off looking at another guy's ass and wanker!"

"It is God's fault I get off lookin' at another guy's ass and wanker!" yelled Marty. "It's yer fault for bein' such a fat, lazy fuck, too fuckin' lazy to get up off yer fat, lazy fuckin' ass!"

"If you being a faggot's God's fault, then why does it say in the Bible that you're going to Hell for buttfucking men?"

"You probably think it's God's fault you get a hard-on every time ya look at a *Happy Meal*," said Marty. "You probably think it's God's fault you can't push yerself away from the fuckin' table! You probably think it's God's fault yer a lazy piece of shit!"

"It ain't God's fault you wanna stick a guy's cock in your mouth," insulted Patrick, "before he sticks it up your ass!"

Once more, Marty slapped Patrick alongside the back of the head. "You just keep yer fuckin' mouth shut about Kris and me, before I kick yer ass from here to Milton Freewater!"

With that, Marty performed some bizarre, improvised dance routine while singing, "'*A minstrel boy to the war is gone, In the ranks of death you will find him*'..."

"What's wrong with those guys?" Billy whispered to Kris.

"What's not wrong with them?" asked Kris, in self-deprecating humor mixed with anger and futility.

"I mean..." Billy shrugged. "I heard some pretty bad language, but nothing like that!"

"Get used to it, Bill. It only gets worse. *A lot worse.*"

"Is that the way they always talk to each other?"

"Pretty much."

"How come?"

Kris smiled. "Because they can."

"But.... Why?"

"You got older brothers, don'tcha?"

"Yeah," answered Billy. "Francis and Carlos."

"Do they ever give you a hard time?"

"Nothing like that!" Billy handed Kris a grape lollipop. "I never seen a family quite like them McKennas."

"That makes two of us," said Kris, placing the lollipop in his mouth.

"All they do is fight, or scream and yell at each other all the time! Papa told me if I ever start cussing like Pat and Marty, he'd thrash me so hard I wouldn't be able to sit down for over a week!"

"Your father's a very good man."

"Pat and Marty get into the worst scrapes," said Billy. "I dunno why they wanna hurt each other so bad, for."

"You can't hurt people like Pat and Marty," said Kris. "Those two can't feel pain. They're too stupid to feel pain."

"Really?" Billy looked up at Kris. "How come?"

Kris laughed. "Because they're Scots and Irish...."

8

The Dirtbags, as Marty called them, lived in one of the last houses on McAlister Lane. After that were farms and orchards, until one got to a travel trailer factory about a mile down the road.

The Moyers' house dated back to the late-Nineteenth Century, and was among the oldest structures in the valley. It was a two-story Victorian, with high ceilings and a steep roof, pointing nearly forty feet above the ground. It was originally built with no electricity or indoor plumbing. It had two fireplaces for wood heat. A bathroom in the rear had been added in the Thirties, and its style didn't match the rest of the building.

The stone foundation was cracking and eroding. This gave the house a lopsided, teetering appearance. The roof was in dire need of repair, and leaked worse than the McKennas' trailer. Air seeped around the doors and windows. The exterior hadn't been painted in recollection. Its once bright blue color faded. A window on the front door had been shattered, and was replaced by plywood. The porch railing had several boards missing.

The lawn had turned to dandelions and morning glory. A beat-up *Dodge Charger* decorated the yard, along with aging washing machines, a cast iron sink, and a couple of upright refrigerators. Beverage cans and bottles and cigarette packages scattered everywhere. The surrounding fence missed pickets, and decaying posts leaned in all directions.

A number of small children, ages ranging from three to preteen, played around the house. They lacked decent clothing, and went barefoot despite the rainy weather. Their teeth were black, crooked, and rotting.

"White trash," whispered Marty, entering the yard through a gate, which dangled from a single hinge. Even trashier than the McKennas, in all their white trash splendor. Grangeford was filled with white trash. But the trashiest of all were the Moyers. No one came that close to being so fucking trashy.

Marty felt as if he stood a bit taller, once he entered the property. He approached the porch with a cockiness bordering on recklessness. He urged himself not to touch anybody or anything, in fear of it rubbing off.

Kris, Patrick, and Billy kept their distances. The Moyers were not nice people, and had the reputation and criminal history to prove it. Kris already feared that coming here was a mistake... a mistake he hoped never to regret.

The younger Moyer children stopped to look at the newcomers. No one stopped to ask their business. Marty, in particular, had his own questionable reputation in the community. To some, Marty was an oddity, a mystery, an enigma...

The Boogie Man.

"If they move, kill 'em," Marty said to Kris, citing a line from *The Wild Bunch*.

Joyce Moyers stepped out of the house, onto the porch. She was nineteen, and one of the Dirtbag's older sisters. She already had two children of her own, and one on the way. All were of different fathers. She was a short, squat, homely little thing with greasy black hair, a face covered with pimples, and a mouthful of bad teeth. She was regarded as an easy piece of tail, even with her appearance.

Joyce bottle-fed one of her children, as a second followed under foot. Wearing a frown, she asked Marty what he wanted.

"Is Michael here?" asked Marty, smiling as he feigned a calm, docile demeanor.

Grangeford was a small town, and Joyce already sort of knew Marty McKenna. She guessed that Marty wasn't there to wish her brother well.

Joyce didn't approve of her brother Mike's attitude or actions. Even then, she thought a lot less of Kris and Marty. Through the rumor mill, she heard that the two were engaged in a lifestyle which were, according to her views, incompatible with rural eastern Oregon or fitting in the eyes of God...a God she didn't especially believe in or worship. "I don't know where Mike is," she said, her tone cold and indifferent. "And I don't know when he'll be back."

Marty gave Joyce two sad, soft eyes. He figured that the Dirtbag and Turtlehead were hiding somewhere in the house. Common sense told him not to pull something stupid, especially not on the Dirtbag turf. Still, he wasn't afraid of the Moyers, even with their greater numbers.

"I think you'd better go," warned Joyce. This wasn't so much of a request, as it was an order.

"Oh?" questioned Marty, still playing the innocent though his wicked grin said otherwise. "And why is that?"

Joyce cleared her throat. "If my dad finds out you're here…"

Too late.

The Head of the Dirtbags, The Patriarch of Grangeford's Lowest of the Low, the Chief Ankle-Biter of All Ankle-Biters….

Floyd Moyers stepped outside, then stood next to Joyce and her youngsters. He was a big man, not only in terms of height but also in a huge belly under a plaid shirt and bib overalls. He was almost sixty, but looked older. His once-dark hair was almost entirely gray now. He revealed thick stubble from a three-day beard, shaded in hues of salt-and-pepper.

Floyd had been a miner, a logger, worked as a janitor and in a hardware store, and raised a dozen kids. Even with advancing age, Floyd and his wife were expecting another kid. Years of using and abusing nicotine, alcohol and weed, along with occasional weekends in jail from drunk driving, theft, and public fights, left him a shell and a shadow of "what might have been". He now spent long days staring at the TV, smoking and drinking and doping and cussing at the world around him.

Floyd's presence sent chills through Billy, Kris, and Patrick. Billy was about to forget all about his video games, take them as a loss, and forget about it.

Marty seemed neither deterred or discouraged by Floyd's arrival. He smiled and stepped toward the older man. "Is Mike here?" he asked, in a folksy manner. "I'd sure like to talk to 'em."

"He ain't here," grunted Floyd, put off by Marty's unwillingness to budge. He glared at the slight figure with the ruffled hair, hooded sweatshirt, and short-short cut-offs. He'd seen Marty before, and refused to believe that some damned queer would dare enter his domain. "You McKenna?" he asked, looking the intruder up one side and down the middle. "Marty McKenna?"

Marty snickered. "Yes, sir."

"The fuck're you doing, coming around here for?" shouted Floyd, stomping out his cigarette as he left the porch to confront Marty. "The fuck gives you the right to come around here, you goddamn little homo?"

Kris, Patrick, and Billy backed away. Not Marty. He stood his ground, as if to welcome a brawl.

This only infuriated Floyd that much more. "Wipe that grin off your face," he snarled. "You goddamn faggot smartass…"

"Take another step closer and I'll tromp you!" threatened Marty, oddly amused at the turmoil he was causing. "Yer son beat the hell outa my brother, then stole Billy's games. You hand them games over, and I'll gladly get the hell outa here, and we'll all be happy."

"Mike didn't take them games," claimed Floyd. "I ain't seen him yet today, and frankly I don't give a shit about your fat-ass brother, your bed-buddy, the little spic you got with ya, or them fucking games. I want you the hell off my place, before…"

"You callin' my fat-ass brother a liar?" snapped Marty, intentionally trying to rile Floyd. "Well, if yer ugly-ass shithead of a son didn't beat Pat up, then steal Billy's games, then who did? The Pillsbury Fuckin' Dough-boy?"

Floyd backhanded Marty's face.

Marty responded, by striking Floyd in the exact same way. "I can go all day, Buckwheat!" he laughed, smiling even though one cheek was red, sore, and stinging, "Can *you?*"

The yard fell deathly quiet as all eyes gazed upon Marty and Floyd. Marty finally broke the silence with a chuckle.

"Get off my place!" screamed Floyd. "Get the fuck outa here right now, or I'll get my 12-guage shotgun and blow your fucking head off!"

"Shotgun?" laughed Marty. "What shotgun? That pea-shooter the cops forgot to confiscate the last time they came to haul you or one of yer asshole kids off to the pokey?"

"*Marty,*" whispered Kris.

"Look, I didn't come here to fight," breathed Marty, a bit more compro-mising. "I come here to get them games back yer kid swiped." He reached into one pocket of his cut-offs for a cell-phone which wasn't there. "Now, are you gonna hand them games over, or do I call the cops, so they'll have to scrounge through that filthy dump t' find 'em?"

"I ain't got a shotgun." admitted Floyd. "But I still got me a shovel and five acres of dirt to bury you in."

"I'm sorry, Mr. Moyers," apologized Kris. "And I'm really sorry for the way Marty's been acting..."

"You're sorry all right, ya goddamn fairy," growled Floyd. "And you're gonna be a damned sight sorrier if ya don't get off my place. Now get!"

"We'll be back," said Marty, grinning. "Even young piglets gotta return to the trough. Mike's gonna have to come back for tonight's feedin'."

"If my boy's got them games, you let me handle it, not you." Floyd pointed at Marty. "Now you get off my place, and don't you come back around here!"

"We're goin'," said Marty, mockingly bowing to Floyd as he stepped away. "Sorry for the way yer kids turned out. But they are yer kids, and one good kid outa twelve ain't bad."

Marty strutted through the gate with Kris, Patrick, and Billy, wearing a self-satisfactory grin.

"Son of a bitch," cursed Floyd. Grudgingly, he stormed back into the house and slammed the door behind him.

* * *

"Gee guys, thanks for all yer help," commented Marty, nearly a hundred yards from the Moyers' house.

"You got a lot of nerve," said Kris. He didn't especially care for the Moyers, for the exception of Lester who succeeded in getting out from under the family's reputation and influence. "I thought he was going to kill us, Marty. I thought he was going to kill us all."

"If I thought he was gonna kill us, you think I woulda confronted him like that?" asked Marty, proud of himself for not backing down. "No worries. His bark's a lot worse'n his bite."

"I thought we was goners!" said Billy.

"You gotta admit, though," said Marty, rubbing his face where Floyd had nailed him. "This sure beats the hell outa boredom."

"Boredom," mumbled Kris. "Boredom beats death, and you have to be alive to get bored."

"Anyway," said Marty. "If Fatrick hadn't got beat up by the Dirtbag, I wouldn't o' risked gettin' my ass whipped on his behalf."

"Fuck you, asshole," responded Patrick.

"'Asshole'?" questioned Marty, slapping the back of Patrick's head. "'Asshole', ya call me? Look at the trouble I gone through to save yer fat ass! Yer my brother, Pat, and I love you! I love you, y' ungrateful son of a bitch! I was willin' to get my ass kicked back there, just like I'm willin' to take one, now. And here you turn around and call me an 'asshole'?"

"That's right, asshole," said Patrick. "Asshole! Irish nigger faggot asshole!"

Kris shook his head in disdain.

"Get it right, shit for brains!" shouted Marty. "The fuckin' Irish are the niggers of Europe! When are you ever gonna get it right? How many times do I gotta tell ya?"

Patrick simply glared at Marty.

"What would you o' done, had ol' Floyd tromped my ass back there?" asked Marty, pointedly.

Patrick smiled. *"Laugh..."*

9

In a quiet neighborhood, the four boys encountered an elderly couple struggling to change the rear-left tire on a *Buick Regal.* Although it wasn't raining, the wind remained damp and chilly.

Marty lit a Camel, took a puff or two, and said nothing.

Kris wondered what entered Marty's thoughts whenever he was uncharacteristically silent. Maybe Marty pondered the Dirtbag and Turtle-head's possible whereabouts. Could be he wanted to return to watching "Red River." Might be he contemplated his own family's issues and woes, while constantly condemning the Moyers for theirs.

Or maybe Marty thought about sex.

That was it...Marty's thoughts involved *sex.*

Marty and Kris approached the older couple. The man had jacked the car part of the way up, then attempted to loosen the nuts with a lug wrench. The jack teetered in the mud and gravel next to the street, and threatened to drop the elevated car to the ground. The old man had neglected to place large stones to the other tires, preventing the car from rolling.

Clearly, the man wasn't in the best of shape. His breath came out as heavy wheezing. Sweat poured from the man's forehead, into his deep-set eyes behind wire-framed glasses. Saliva dripped from his well-trimmed, gray mustache. As the man knelt to the ground, his once-clean slacks were stained and dirty. He leaned into the car, fighting to stabilize his wobbly feet.

His wife was a tiny, frail, birdlike woman, whose height barely reached five feet. She could only grant her husband moral support. Her joints hurt constantly, due to the harsh weather. Had she tried to assist her husband, the woman would've only harmed herself.

Pride and necessity motivated the man to change the tire. Advancing age, prior heart surgeries, and declining health were his greatest enemies. Years before, the chore of changing a tire would've meant nothing. The humility and distress in the man's face were all-too-apparent.

Without asking to do so, Marty helped the man to his feet. He then crouched down to loosen the remaining nuts. Meanwhile, Kris jacked the car up higher, as Patrick and Billy found rocks to place against the other tires.

"You don't have to do this," the man apologized. He used a handkerchief to remove sweat from his face, then wiped his muddy hands. "I sure hate being such a bother to ya..."

"No bother," said Marty, carefully resting the nuts into a hubcap, next to the car. "Why hell, I love changin' tires!"

That was a lie. In truth, Marty hated changing tires, and thought even less of automobiles. He was an avid walker, and saw need in cars for primarily long distances. However, he wouldn't tolerate the sight of an older couple in dire straits.

Marty hastily went about changing the tire. This, despite getting his hands and bare legs filthy from the rain-soaked ground. Marty smiled and hummed Danny Boy as he removed the flat tire from its wheel.

"Got a spare?" asked Kris.

The old man handed Kris the trunk keys.

As Kris fetched the spare tire from the trunk, the old man smiled admirably at those which he regarded as decent, honorable young men. "Boy, I sure hate to see you fellas have to do my work for me," he said.

"Well, we hate to see you get so muddy and worn out from it," responded Kris, helping Marty slip the spare tire to the wheel.

"Can't thank you fellas enough," the man said. He failed to look Marty and Kris in the eyes, and cursed himself from shame.

"Aw, no need to thank us," said Marty, brushing off his hands, clothes, and legs. "Glad we got here when we did."

The man reached into his wallet for two twenties.

"You don't owe us a thing," said Kris.

"But look at yourselves!" the woman cried. "We just hate seeing you lads get so black and blue, on our behalf!"

"It ain't nothin'," claimed Marty, pouring on the charm. "Why, if I can't help someone else out once in a while, may the good Lord strike me dead!"

"We wish," whispered Patrick.

"Buy you fellas each a burger?" the man offered.

Initially, Kris and Marty turned the offer down. The man refused to take 'no' as an answer. At any rate, it was past noon, and the younger boys complained of their empty stomachs.

Finally, Kris and Marty took the older man up on his kindness and generosity. "Ever been to the OK Corral?" asked Marty, as he and the other lads crowded into the back seat of the Buick.

"If it's in the same place it was, fifty years ago," the man said, starting the car and pulling away.

"Dunno where else it'd be," laughed Marty.

"I'm Abigail Thatcher," the woman said to her passengers. "This is my husband, Barry."

"I'm Martin McKenna," said Marty, shaking Abigail's hand. "Just call me 'Marty'."

"Or something else," joked Patrick.

 This here's my kid brother *Fatrick*," Marty went on, giving his sibling the evil eye. "His chum Billy Rodriquez." Marty threw one arm around Kris' shoulders. "And this is my best friend, Kristoffer English."

"Glad to meet you," said Barry, turning a right onto Main Street.

Barry and Abigail examined the businesses and structures of downtown Grangeford, in wistful awe and nostalgia. "Old place stayed just about the same," commented Barry, with a hint of melancholy. "Only the faces and the cars have changed. And my hair."

"Barry and I grew up in Grangeford," said Abigail, proudly. "Went clear through high school here."

"That's cool," said Kris, hoping not to wear out his welcome.

"Spent a couple or three years in the Corps," said Barry. "Soon as I got out, Abby and me moved to Klamath Falls, where I went to Oregon Tech. Got me a job at a machine shop in Salem. Ain't hardly been back to Grangeford since.... Till now."

"Wow!" shouted Billy, as Patrick released a whistle in astonishment. "That's an awful long time!"

"Only when you add up the years, son," said Barry.

Abigail snickered.

"You were in the Marine Corps?" asked Marty.

"Yes, sir," said Barry. "Radio operator in 'Nam, when it was just a police action and not a war."

"That's honorable," complimented Kris.

"Didn't think so at the time," said Barry. "Didn't think too much of 'Nam. Ain't the good ol' U S of A, even if that's what they tried to make it. Before then they tried to make it part of France."

"France," muttered Marty, disparagingly. "Aw, well. Them Frogs do make a couple of good movies, now and then."

"Only good thing about 'Nam was the nooky," laughed Barry, "and even it wasn't all that good."

"Barry!" scolded Abigail, giving her husband a good-natured nudge on the shoulder.

"Ain't no nooky like Yankee nooky!" laughed Barry, glancing through the rearview mirror at Kris and Marty. "Whadda you fellas gotta say about it?"

Marty giggled as Kris nervously loosened his collar.

"Left here about fifty, sixty years ago," said Barry, contemplating the changes that Grangeford had went through. "Always talked about coming back for a visit, or maybe to stay. Never have."

"Only when your mother passed away, fifteen years ago," said Abigail. "And we only stayed for the funeral. Showed up for the service, had coffee at a roadside diner, then headed home to Salem."

"That's right," whispered Barry, vacantly.

"Is your mom buried in the cemetery, back yonder?" asked Marty.

"That she is, son," answered Barry. "We had just left there, before we got the flat."

"Me and Kris go into the boneyard, once in a while," said Marty. "We can spend hours there just checkin' out the names on the headstones, talk about our lives together, and *other stuff*." Marty grinned mischievously as he patted Kris' leg, just above the knee. "Ain't that right, Kristoffer?"

Kris elbowed Marty's ribs, as his face reddened in a blush.

The older couple gave Kris and Marty suspicious stares, but said nothing.

Moments later, the Buick pulled in front of the *OK Corral*, and stopped. Everyone entered the diner. Barry and Abigail looked all around the diner's interior, as if to gaze upon the face of an old friend. Barry motioned for Abigail to the ceiling fans above, as well as a pop machine in one corner. "They weren't here when we left," he said. "Otherwise, everything's just about the same, I swear…Same color paint on the walls and everything."

"Who knows," said Marty, marching through the diner like he owned the joint. "Might be the exact same paint, for all I know."

"I declare," whispered Abigail, fighting back the sadness of lost years.

Mark McKenna rushed to his newest customers, carrying a platter with glasses of water, silverware, and menus. He was a bit concerned when he saw Billy and Kris, along with his two brothers, accompanying an elderly couple. Perhaps Marty had arranged the sale of oceanfront property in Arizona.

Mark motioned everyone to a long table in the center of the dining room, then asked if they wanted coffee.

"A cup of joe for Abby and me," said Barry. "And get what these boys want, on my dime."

"Coming right up!" said Mark. He reached the kitchen door, then motioned for Marty to join him.

Marty did what he was told.

"What's going on?" asked Mark.

"Whadda ya mean?" questioned Marty.

"Who are those folks with you, Marty?"

"Barry and Abigail," smirked Marty.

Mark gritted his teeth. "And just who are Barry and Abigail, smartass?"

"Nice people."

"Goddamn you, Marty!"

"We changed their tire," explained Marty, "so they're paying us back."

"That's good," sighed Mark. "There for a moment, I thought you were up to something."

"What would I be up to? Five-three? Five-four?"

"*Hardy-har-har.*"

"All we did was change their tire," said Marty. "So, they're paying us back. That's all."

"You and Patrick watch your language," urged Mark. "*Please?*"

Marty grinned.

"You ever catch up with Mike Moyers?" asked Mark. "Or as you call him…the *Dirtbag?*"

"Naw, but it's early yet."

"Ya know, I been thinking. Might be best for the police to handle this. Why take the law into your own hands?"

"Why the fuck not?" argued Marty. "All the cops are gonna do is slap the Dirtbag's slimy little hands, wag their fingers at 'em, tell 'em never to do it again, then let the sorry prick go."

"Yeah, but..."

"The Dirtbag's got sticky fingers! You can't tell people like that not to steal! They was born that way. Chances are, a turd like that's gonna die a thief, unless I kill 'em first. Just our luck, he's too fuckin' stupid to die."

"Yeah, just like the McKennas," commented Mark. "Just like all re-tarded Micks. Best thing is for Pat to tell the cops what happened to him. Hopefully, they'll get Billy's games back."

"If the Dirtbag's still got 'em. Bet he sold the fuckin' things to buy dope. Best way to handle the son of a bitch is to let me kick the shit outa him."

"Well, chances are he'll end up doing something else stupid. By the time he's eighteen, he'll be in the state pen." Mark patted Marty's shoulder. "I better get back to work, or find me another job after I get canned for talking to you. But whatever you do, Marty, make sure it ain't something stupid. Please?"

"Aw, c'mon man!" laughed Marty. "You know me better'n that!"

"I do, Marty," said Mark, no jest in his voice, "and that's what scares me..."

10

Kris sat next to Abigail. He quietly sipped his Coke and observed Barry, who discussed his years in the Marine Corps prior to getting an education at Oregon Tech. Barry then spent thirty-five years manufacturing widgets, sprockets, thing-a-ma-jigs and do-hickies, to attach onto other widgets, sprockets, thing-a-ma-jigs and do-hickies.

Barry and Abigail bought a lovely, modest home in the suburbs, where they raised two boys and a girl. Barry worked in a factory, as Abigail found employment in a few grocery stores and restaurants, along with an artists' co-op. They were now empty-nesters, and enjoyed retirement.

The Thatchers long discussed spending a few days visiting Grangeford. During their first day back, they got a flat tire, then found themselves making friends with "four good boys".

Abigail leaned over to Kris and said, "Barry's the first and only man I ever loved. I've been in love with him for more than sixty years!"

Kris smiled. "That's cool."

"He was so handsome when he was your age!" bragged Abigail. "And he's still very handsome. Don't you agree?"

Kris chuckled.

"Well, you're very handsome too!" laughed Abigail.

"Thanks!"

"You're also a very gentle person. I have two boys, and I can tell."

"I try," said Kris, flattered by the compliment.

"Something tells me you're going to make some lucky girl very happy," giggled Abigail.

Kris turned away from Abigail. She meant no harm by what she said. She was just a nice woman, saying nice things to a nice kid, in a very nice manner.

Kris admired the Thatchers for their love and commitment. Sixty years...What an amazing stretch! Sixty years, three children, and a home in the suburbs. The good life.

No doubt, Barry and Abigail had their tough times, too. Somehow, they worked out their differences and stuck it out.

Being totally unaware of it, Kris found himself staring at Marty, who chatted with Barry on the other end of the table. Kris loved Marty, and was attracted to him. He sure didn't like everything about Marty, but who did? Marty was Marty, and that's about all anyone could say about it. Marty was Marty. And Kris loved Marty, no matter what... while hoping that Marty loved him with the same love and devotion.

Kris eyed Marty's slight frame, imagining what he might look like in sixty-years, assuming Marty lived that long. Would Kris and Marty manage to stay together that long, or would their differences eventually separate them? Did they stand a chance of becoming a married couple? What would it be like to enjoy dinner with Marty, each and every night, or to make love with him each and every night, fall asleep in his arms and then wake up next to him? Would their love survive as well as the Thatchers'? Or was their relationship doomed, even before they left high school?

There were always other fish in the sea.

"Is there someone very special in your life?" Abigail asked Kris.

"Yes," said Kris, unable to look Abigail in the eyes. "I think...I hope.... I believe there is. I can only hope he feels the same about me, as I do for him..."

"'Him'?" Abigail's mouth dropped open. "'*Him*'?"

Kris gasped, as panic swept over his entire body. His first impulse was to flee from the *OK Corral*, away from Abigail's sight, attitudes, and judgment. He feared from going totally insane.

Abigail shot a glance at Marty, then at Kris.

Kris grew ill. Carelessly, foolishly, stupidly, he let the cat out of the bag, and Abigail was onto him. Kris' face got red, and he nearly wept.

Barry had no clue what Kris and Abigail were chatting about. He was too busy sharing stories about his escapades in a Saigon poontang palace with the other boys.

"I have a nephew named Kolby," Abigail whispered discreetly, making sure Barry was oblivious to what she said to Kris. "Barry doesn't like Kolby because... well, because he's like you. But he's a wonderful boy, my Kolby!"

Kris slumped. He looked deeply into Abigail's eyes, seeking her approval and understanding.

Abigail nearly choked up. Somehow, she managed to keep her emotions in check. "Kolby's a fine boy, just like I know you're a fine boy!" she told Kris. "And I pray that you'll be just as happy spending your life with that special someone, no matter who *he* is. I pray that you'll find as much happiness in your life as I have with my Barry!"

11

Everyone enjoyed their coffee, Cokes and burgers, and engaged in relaxing conversation.

By two in the afternoon, Barry and Abigail paid for the meals, then left to visit old friends. The four boys wished them well, and soon resumed their search for the Dirtbag and Turtlehead.

Rain put a stop to their effort. The four boys found themselves in a narrow alley, tucked between empty, desolate warehouses, a couple of taverns, and an Asian cuisine. The tinny music of country music from a jukebox blared out of the open door of a saloon. Occasionally, drunkards stepped from the backdoor, walking sideways as they'd give the boys crooked smiles then meander into the wet weather.

The rain came down in buckets. Kris wanted to either return to the OK Corral, or better yet to his Aunt Barbara's. He preferred forgetting all about the Dirtbag and Turtlehead. Like Mark, Kris thought it best to let the cops deal with the theft of Billy's games.

Marty despised the Dirtbag and Turtlehead with a passion. He hated them that much more for what they did to Patrick and Billy. Even then, Kris wondered if Marty's sole purpose had nothing to do with payback, but rather a way to get into a fight, just for the hell of it. Hardly a week went by where he didn't get himself into a scrape. If a troublemaker didn't want to tangle, then Marty went out of his way to push them into it...and usually made quick work of it.

Marty could sure take one helluva punch! Kris saw him get struck so hard, as if to floor a horse or a mule. Somehow, Marty managed to remain on his feet, then nail an antagonist twice as hard. He'd come out of a fight bloodied and bruised, all right. No matter. He always came out on top.

Still, Marty's willingness to fight always scared Kris. Eventually, Marty would meet his match, get left in a gutter or (*worse yet!*) in a hospital or (*worse yet!*) in a morgue.

Marty was no pretty boy. Nor was he homely. He was rough around the edges, and scruffy. He walked most everywhere, and stayed in shape. In Kris' opinion, Marty's legs were the best eye candy around! The last thing Kris wanted was to see Marty get thrashed so badly, where he wasn't attractive.

The four boys stood under the eve of an abandoned brick building, waiting for the rain to stop. The alley was cluttered with debris, as stray cats and dogs scrounged through dumpsters and garbage cans for discarded food. A Glad bag filled with fish heads and guts had been ripped open, and the smell was atrocious.

The four boys said little. Their grim, hangdog expressions said it all. Thunder rumbled from overhead, and echoed throughout the streets and corridors of town.

The monotony was broken when Marty said, "Hey, Kris, let's tell Fatrick and Billy t' get lost, so we can take our pants off and partake in the old fuck and suck."

Patrick roared in laughter, while Billy gasped in shock.

"Why do you always say those things?" protested Kris.

"What things?" asked Marty.

"'Partake in the old fuck and suck'," repeated Kris, embarrassed because Patrick and Billy were there to hear it.

"Would you rather stand here all fuckin' day, waiting for the rain to stop pissin' on us?" questioned Marty, keeping a straight face though he was on the verge of smirking. "Gotta pass the time o' day somehow, before I beat the shit outa two deserving assholes."

Kris shook his head and sighed.

"What?" asked Marty, acting all offended because Kris acted all offended.

"I don't know about you sometimes, Marty," mumbled Kris.

"What don't you know about me, *Kristoffer?*"

"I don't understand why you always say such dirty things to me!"

"They're not dirty," said Marty. "All I asked is if ya wanted to lose yer pants so we can prop ourselves on one of these garbage cans and have some fun."

"Look, we're not doing the 'fuck and suck' on one of these filthy garbage cans!" screamed Kris. "We're not about to do the 'fuck and suck' anywhere in public! Keep it up, Marty, and we'll never 'fuck and suck'! Got it?"

"Keep what up?" whined Marty, in false astonishment.

Kris glared at Marty. "The whole wide world doesn't need to know about us!"

"'Know'? 'Know' what?"

"You know." Kris' eyes dampened. "About *us*."

"Faggots," whispered Patrick.

Marty laughed. "This may come as a shock to ya, but it's not much of a secret in town. People already know we're an item. Everyone knows we're gay, homosexuals, deviants, faggots, queers, daisies, perverts, butt fuckers, cocksuckers, taint lickers..."

Patrick giggled.

"*Marty!*" shrieked Kris.

"I love you, Kristoffer Daniel English," said Marty, uncharacteristically serious. "Goddamn it, I don't care what others gotta say about it, or if they even like us! I love you, Kris! Why should I be ashamed of who I am, or of what we are?"

"I just don't want everyone knowing it," explained Kris. "That's all."

"I don't give a fuck if everyone knows it or not! Why should I fuckin' care? It ain't gonna change the way I am, or how I feel about you. I love ya, man, and I wanna be with you! Yer the one makin' a fuckin' crime outa it, not me!"

"But you make it sound so criminal!" argued Kris. "It's not what you say that bothers me. It's how you say it."

Marty chuckled. "You mean the 'fuck and suck' thing."

Kris didn't answer. His wounded expression said it all.

"Damn it, Kris!" laughed Marty. "You know me better'n that! I don't mean nothin' by it. It's just my sense o' humor."

"It's not funny," griped Kris.

"Aw, I dunno," said Marty. "Least we're not out here, bored out of our wits."

"There's no danger of that with you," said Kris. "Is there?"

"I aim to please!" snickered Marty.

"The only reason people know about us is because of you and your big mouth on *Facebook*," said Kris, glaring suspiciously at Patrick. "Or *him*."

Patrick shook his head in denial.

"I wish everyone could mind their own business," mumbled Kris, in resentment.

"Or learn to live with it," said Marty. "We ain't the problem, Kris. No one said that everybody's gonna like us, or even learn to accept us."

At that very moment, Marty caught sight of E McKenna, stepping outside of the tavern's backdoor for a smoke.

E was Mark, Patrick, and Marty's mother. "E" stood for *Emily*, a name the woman absolutely hated and refused to answer to. She was forty, but looked older due to premature graying hair, missing teeth, baggy eyes, and a wrinkled brow.

E rarely changed her clothes. Already, her tank top and holey jeans were sweaty and soiled. No telling how long she'd been in that particular tavern. Based upon the smell of her breath, and her teetering walk, she arrived minutes after getting out of bed. E rarely ate, and usually sustained herself on the nuts and pretzels which bar patrons snacked on. She was slightly taller than Marty, as skinny as a rail, and gaunt. Her skin was pale and oily.

E smiled as she saw two of her sons standing next to some garbage cans across the alley. She called and waved them both over.

Patrick sprinted to give E a hug and a kiss.

Marty was conflicted when it came to his mother. E was beautiful when she was much younger. As time passed by, the woman grew increasingly grotesque as a lifestyle of nicotine, weed, and liquor took a toll on her. Marty was disgusted with E, and even more put off by whatever piece of shit guy she picked up at bars...guys destined to become Losers of the Month.

The present Loser of the Month was Lance. He wasn't the lousiest of the Losers, but for damned sure wasn't the best. On a scale from one-to-ten, ten being sort of okay or even kind of cool, and one being a total ass-wipe, Lance was a four or five. Marty hoped that Lance's status of being Loser of the Month was brief. He respected very few of the Losers, and generally disliked them that much more. Still, Lance bathed once in a while, and sometimes brushed all three of his decaying teeth.

E was Marty's mom...wasn't she? She was the only mother he had, and ever would have.

Marty loved E. He loved her, whether he wanted to or not. The harder it was to love E, the more Marty wished to love her. And the more Marty wanted E to quit the booze and the drugs and the Losers of the Month, the more he wanted her to visit a dentist, sober up, and find a fucking job.

There was still hope... wasn't there?

Marty slowly went to greet E. He didn't rush over like Patrick. Instead, he meandered, sauntered and strutted. He tried to look cool and in control, even as his thoughts for E overwhelmed him.

Marty's conflicted feelings and emotions nearly got the better of him, and he nearly wept. Teen swagger and bravado held it back. Once Marty wrapped both arms around E's waist, he nearly lost it.

He got over it, once he heard the first words out of E's mouth. "Oh honey," she begged. "You wouldn't have a few bucks I could borrow?"

Marty frowned. *Typical.* He worked a few hours a week at the *OK Corral*, washing dishes, swabbing the deck, sweeping the sidewalk, grating hashbrowns, and cleaning the shitters. It gave him a little money to buy a burger, go to the movies, purchase a cheap DVD, and be a kid. It also helped Mark pay some of the bills, such as electricity and propane. Unfortunately, it also helped support E's fucked-up lifestyle and habits.

Although Marty swore that he'd never do it again, he found himself digging through his wallet to hand E an *Alexander Hamilton.* He resented the stupid-ass smile on his face as he planted the money in E's possession.

"What about a smoke?" requested E, carrying a noticeable lisp through her missing teeth.

Marty grudgingly offered E a pack of Camels, then lit one for himself. The cigarette was relaxing and soothing. It contrasted with images running through Marty's head, mainly strangling E until she died or grew a fucking brain in that thick skull of hers.

"What have you been up to, honey?" E asked Marty.

Marty told E about the Dirtbag beating Patrick up, then swiping Billy's games.

"Oh, I'm so sorry!" whined E, embracing both Patrick and Billy. She looked them up one side and down the other, making sure they were all right and not permanently scarred or disabled.

"I'm a'right," said Patrick, turning his head to avoid the smell of beer fuming from E's mouth. "I'm just kinda mad, that's all."

"But did he hurt you?" asked E, in genuine concern.

"Pat's okay," said Marty. "The Dirtbag and Turtlehead won't be, soon as I catch up with 'em."

"*Marty,*" scolded E.

Marty snickered.

E gave Patrick another embrace, then a wet smooch on the cheek. "Run along, honey," she said. "There's something I gotta talk to Marty about."

"A'right," agreed Patrick. "Love ya, Mom!"

Marty sighed. He had no idea what E wished to chat with him about, but already knew he wouldn't like it.

"Lance wants to move in with us," said E, hoping this announcement didn't upset Marty.

Marty peeked into the tavern to see Lance belly-up to the bar, telling lies about working on oil rigs throughout the United States, Canada, Mexico, South America, and the Middle East. It was bullshit. Lance never did such work. The closest he ever came to an oil rig was viewing Marty's DVD of *There Will Be Blood,* if the mouthy son of a bitch was even sober enough to recall it.

Lance was between jobs, bumming off those foolish enough to loan him a buck. He migrated from a couch in his parents' home to E's bed at the McKennas'. Lance increasingly spent more time at E's, a point not lost when Marty said, "I thought he was a'ready livin' with us, Mom."

"Well, he sorta is," said E, noting the sour look on Marty's face. "Permanent, I mean"

"Okay," groaned Marty, though there was nothing okay in the way he said it.

Silence wedged Marty and E. Finally, E whispered, "I'm also asking Mark to move out."

Marty gasped.

"Mark's a grown man!" cried E. "He... he's a grown man, and I can't see why he's insisting on staying..."

"Mark's the only reason we're survivin'!" shrieked Marty. "If it wasn't for him payin' most o' the fuckin' bills, our asses would be freezin' in the dark!"

"Lance and Mark don't like each other," explained E. "And I just figured..."

"Who the fuck says I like Lance?" argued Marty.

"Marty!"

"Ain't we got enough problems without you invitin' some lazy-assed jerk in the house? While ya spend every fuckin' dime you got in some shithole dive like this?"

"It's none of your fucking business what I do with my money!" yelled E.

"It is my business when ya let piles of shit move in with us!"

Kris remained across the alley, watching this exchange. Marty and E couldn't be in the same room without a fight. Kris used to involve himself into their squabbles. Past experiences now urged him to stay free from them. It didn't prevent him from feeling lousy.

"Goddamn you, Marty McKenna!" cursed E. "Lance ain't no pile of shit!"

"The fuck he ain't, Mom!" Marty shouted back. "The goddamned motherfuck he ain't!"

"If that's the way you think, then why don't you up and move the fuck out, too? You think you're old enough to take care of yourself, mister?"

"It's pretty fuckin' obvious you ain't!" responded Marty.

This wasn't the first time E kicked Marty out. Over the past year or so, Marty usually crashed at Aunt Barbara's with Kris for a couple of nights, until E arrived to make peace. Mother and son would have a tearful reconciliation, make an amends, then coexist until the next blow-up. Well, mother and son were overdue for a blow-up. As always, Kris was there to play witness to it.

"Anywhere I end up can't be worse than where I am now!" snapped Marty, knowingly pushing his luck.

"Then why don't you pack all your shit up and fucking do it?" questioned E.

Marty lowered his head in fear, frustration, and anxiety. It always hurt him to get into disputes with E. "Mom," he whimpered. "Didn't you promise me you were gonna quit drinkin'?"

E was about to make a snide comment, but was stopped dead in her tracks.

"And ain't you supposed to be goin' to them AA meetings?" added Marty, his voice hoarse and raspy.

"I'm trying!" claimed E. "Believe me, I'm trying."

"Mom!"

"It's not that easy, Marty!"

"Mom," urged Marty. "Whatever ya do, please don't throw Mark out. If ya throw anyone out, throw Lance out."

"But I love Lance!"

"Well, I sure the fuck don't!"

"You won't give him a chance, Marty!" screamed E.

"I want to! But he don't like me, he don't like my old movies, and he don't like Kris!"

"He likes you! It's just that...He doesn't understand you."

"He don't like Kris and me 'cause he don't like what we are!" yelled Marty.

"He's never been around guys like Kris and you," explained E, shrugging. "Lance spent his entire life working on jobs..."

"Workin' on jobs with *real* men, not queer-boys like Kris and me!" assumed Marty, sarcastically. "He's only been around real men, workin' real jobs! Is that what you mean?"

"Marty...."

"If them jobs are only for *real* men," added Marty, "then why the fuck're they hirin' a piece o' shit like him?"

E slapped Marty's face.

Then Marty slapped E across her left cheek, as hard as he could, in the exact same manner. "Gonna have to learn to hit harder!" he laughed, considering the grief it brought him. "That is, if ya want my attention!"

"Get the fuck out!" demanded E, in a shrill voice. "Just get the fuck out! Get all of your shit the fuck outa my house, and move your sorry little Irish ass the fuck out! Move the fuck out, and never come back!"

"I'll move the fuck out, a'right! I'll move the fuck out, me and Mark both! Then you and Sir Lance-A-Fuck are gonna be in a world o' shit when they shut the power and heat off!"

E kicked wildly at Marty's bare shins. This ended when Marty slugged E, right on the nose.

E took a couple of clumsy steps back, and nearly toppled over. The only thing preventing her from falling on her backside was the tavern's brick wall. Even then, E required a moment or two to bounce back from the impact of Marty's attack. "Fucking bastard!" she shrieked, as loud as she could. "Goddamn fucking bastard!"

"Want me t' do it again?" dared Marty, grinning like a crazy man. "A'right, then bring it on! Bring it!"

"Son of a bitch!" cursed E, sprinting into the tavern.

"Let's get out of here!" urged Kris.

Marty sighed. Slowly, gradually, he calmed down. "Yeah, Kris," he admitted, in shame and humility. "Let's get goin'. I better head on home, start cleanin' all my shit out..."

"So, I'm a piece of shit?" someone spoke, from the tavern door.

Kris and Marty turned to see Lance stepping outside.

Lance was a thin, scrawny, sweaty man in his early-forties. Unruly strands of hair dotted his face, a pathetic attempt at growing facial hair. Both fists were clenched. He strutted toward the two boys, like he was the toughest dude around. He believed his mere presence was enough to force Marty into backing down, apologize to E, and act like a man for once.

Lance was taller than Marty (*who wasn't?*) and nearly as tall as Kris. He carried little weight. His arms were stringy and boney. He wore a greasy, yellow tee-shirt, baggy sweat pants, and leather sandals.

"What kind of a man hits his own mother?" growled Lance. "Tell me that. Tell me! What kind of a man hits his own mother?"

"Keep away from me," ordered Marty, standing his ground as Kris stepped away. "Keep yer fuckin' mouth shut about me and Mom. And while yer at it, keep yer fuckin' mouth shut about Kris and me."

"Make me," demanded Lance. "Go ahead, Marty. Make me! Big man, ain'tcha? *Huh?* Real big man, ain'tcha? Real big pussy, that's all."

"You ain't my dad," Marty said. "You ain't my dad, so don't act like it."

"And you ain't no son to me. Wouldn't claim you if you was. No son of mine would hit his own mother!"

Marty wasn't afraid of Lance. Even then, Lance's comments cut Marty clear to the bone. Marty felt terrible about striking E. But someone had to strike her...Right? Someone had to knock some sense into her, get her off the booze and the weed and out of the fucking bars! Maybe now she'll clean up, visit a dentist, then get a fucking job and become a better mom, like she was supposed to be.

Right?

Right?

Marty whimpered, and he fought back tears. His emotions were almost too great a burden.

"Sawed-off chickenshit," taunted Lance. "Admit it. You're nothing but a mouthy, sawed-off little chickenshit. You can hit women. Care to try it with me?"

"Leave me the fuck alone, Lance," said Marty. "Do us a big favor. Go sponge off o' yer mommy and daddy. That is, if they can even stand bein' around you. Fuckin' stoner."

"Get your ass over here so I can knock your teeth down your throat," threatened Lance. "Too scared, ain'tcha Marty? Too scared to fight me! Yeah, you can hit your mother, but not me! Stand there, acting all rough and tough for your fuck-buddy when we both know you're shitting yourself. You can hit women. Care to take a swing at me, punk? A real man? Care to hit me?"

"You ain't a real man."

"Neither are you," snickered Lance. "Real men don't suck dick or hump other guys. Just as well you're queer. Real women would never take an interest in a coward like you."

Marty grew increasingly angrier, as guilt and shame overtook him. Yeah, it was a pretty lousy thing, striking E! Already, Marty wanted to make an amends with her, regardless of who was at fault. Pride got in the way.

Pride always got in the way.

"Let's go, Marty," urged Kris. "C'mon. Let's just go."

"That's right, Marty," giggled Lance. "You and Kris run away and hide, like the two queer-boys you truly are."

"I might be a queer-boy." Marty grinned, maliciously. "But I ain't a lazy fuckin' stoner, like you."

Lance and Marty glared at each other, for several seconds. In the distance, the cry of a fire engine sounded through the rain, fog, and haze.

"Do what E told you," ordered Lance. "Get you and your shit outa the house, and don't let me catch you coming back around. You ain't welcome there no more. Only thing you oughta know, Marty. Ain't near as much of your shit in the bedroom, as there was."

"Fuck are you talkin' about?" questioned Marty, the hairs on the back of his head bristling. "Just what the fuck are you talkin' about?"

"After you left this morning," said Lance, "your mom and me boxed up all your movies and your DVD player and hauled them to a fucking pawn shop."

Marty sent a fist into Lance's nose.

The grin on Lance's face was replaced by expressions of astonishment, fear, and shock. His eyes widened. His mouth gaped open, and blood shot from his shattered nose.

The next few seconds were dreamlike, darkly humorous, and surreal, as if they derived from the darkest realms of a troubled mind, or a Sam Peckinpah movie.

Lance flew backwards. His arms and legs extended in the shape of an X. He collided into a half-dozen garbage cans, which toppled over and scattered like bowling pins.

Lance remained motionless, in the muddy debris. Trash spilled into the alleyway, where it got drenched in the rain. Lance was dazed, baffled, and confused. He looked up to see Marty stepping toward him, carrying a thirty-three-gallon, steel garbage can. Awkwardly, he shoved his arms out, to divert Marty.

"Fuckin' pile o' shit!" cursed Marty, whacking Lance with the garbage can.

Lance screamed.

Marty struck Lance, over and over and over again, with the garbage can. "Motherfuckin', cocksuckin', asshole son of a bitch!" he shrieked. "Hope you fuckin' die, ya sorry son of a bitch! Motherfuckin', cocksuckin' asshole!"

"Marty!" called Kris.

Marty wasn't easily swayed. Even as Kris managed to yank the garbage can away from him, he still had his feet. Muddy footprints from his thrift shop *Adidas* smashed into Lance's head, arms, legs, crotch, and belly.

Kris lifted Marty and threw him across the alley. Marty landed hard on his butt, in the pouring rain. Patrick and Billy looked on with amazement, admiration, awe, pleasure, and delight.

"Enough, Marty!" shouted Kris. "Enough! He's had enough!"

"The fuck he has!" argued Marty. "I'm just fuckin' gettin' started!"

"Get a grip on yourself," said Kris, "before you hurt someone!"

Marty was too upset to respond in a volley of insults. He merely sat there in the rain, as tears drained from both eyes. Finally, he got to his feet, then sprinted away through the storm and wet alleys of Grangeford.

"Marty!" exclaimed Kris. "Come back!"

It did no good. Seconds later, Marty was more than a hundred yards away from the others. Kris, Patrick, and Billy pursued him, as the rain now came down in buckets.

Three blocks away, they found Marty crouched in the back corner of a Mexican restaurant, bawling like he lost everything which mattered to him.

Kris cautiously approached Marty, as the younger boys kept their distance. "Marty," he whispered, kneeling to his dearest friend and confidante. He softly placed one hand on Marty's thigh. "*Marty?*"

"Fucker took all my movies to a pawn shop!" wept Marty, his words muffled under both hands. "Motherfucker took all my movies to a fuckin' pawn shop!"

"Are you so sure about that?" questioned Kris. He sat next to Marty in the corner, concealed from the damp by a tin roof which the restaurant added on to allow customers and employees a place to smoke. "You so sure about that, Marty? Maybe he just said that to hurt you."

Marty cuddled against Kris, allowing the tears to flow freely. He tried to speak, but it came out as whines and gibberish.

"Pat," whispered Kris, motioning the younger boys over. "Billy?"

Patrick and Billy slowly wandered toward Kris and Marty.

"Run on home," Kris told Patrick. "Go see if Marty's movies are there."

Patrick didn't budge.

"Pat," spoke Kris, sternly. "Run home and see if Marty's movies are still there."

"What's in it for me?" asked Patrick, deviously.

Kris reached into his wallet for a ten. "Is that good enough?" he asked, tiredly. "Or do you want me to kiss your butt, too?"

"Make it twenty," said Patrick, "and maybe I'll run faster."

"I doubt it," said Kris, offering Patrick another ten. "Run on home and see if Marty's movies are still there. Please? Pretty please?"

Patrick snickered.

"Try to find a box in all that...*stuff* you guys have piled everywhere," said Kris. "Then take Marty's movies to my Aunt Barbara's, for safe keeping."

"Okay," agreed Patrick, as he and Billy did as they were told.

"It's all right," said Kris, gently caressing Marty's face and hair. "It's all right, I promise."

"Kris," sobbed Marty. "Why's me and my family so fucked up? *Why?*"

Kris shrugged.

"Everything's fucked up," whined Marty. "Life's fucked up, my family's fucked up. I'm fucked up! Everything's so goddamned fucked up! Everything!"

"No, Marty, not everything..."

"Bullshit! The whole fuckin' world's nothin' but a big suck-ass cock, and there ain't nothin' we can do about it!"

"It doesn't have to be that way," said Kris, searching for the words to not only to help Marty, but to sooth his own anxieties. "Just think. One day we'll leave this ugly little town so we can live together, be together, and stay together. Always! Life doesn't have to be so... screwed up. Someday, you and I can live together, somewhere no one knows us, where they can't judge us, or talk shit..."

"Some days, I just don't wanna live," mumbled Marty, wiping his dampened eyes. "Some days I wish I wasn't here. I wish I was dead!"

"Don't say that," sighed Kris. "If you were dead, I'd want to be dead too!"

Marty rested his head against Kris' chest. In one ear, he heard the beating of Kris' heart. "Fuck," he spoke, softly. "If it wasn't for my movies, or my brother Mark..." He looked into Kris' eyes. "Or if it wasn't for you... Fuck, man! I couldn't make it!" Marty rubbed his hand to Kris' cheek, then kissed him on the lips. "Don't leave me," he begged, his voice high-pitched and raspy. "Whatever ya do, don't you dare fuckin' leave me!"

Kris was on the verge of losing it.

"I love you," said Marty, biting his bottom lip. "I might not always say it, and I might not always think it. But I love you! Don't you dare fuckin' leave me, Kris! I love you!"

"I love you too, Marty!" Kris kissed Marty's forehead. "I love you so very, very much!"

Kris and Marty embraced.

Marty locked lips with Kris. As one hand glided through Kris' hair, the other rubbed his knee and thigh. Thunder rumbled from up above, as a heavy downpour of rain continued to soak Grangeford.

Kris and Marty relished this moment of silence and solitude, protected by a small, tin eve hanging from the back of a Mexican restaurant. Openly, they expressed love and compassion, free from suspicious, cruel minds, or spiteful judgment of those unwilling to accept them. Kris and Marty vowed to spend their lives together, as a strong, unified force. Expressions of undying devotion carried more truth and meaning than words possibly could.

Despite the wind and the rain and explosive thunder, Kris and Marty kept each other safe, warm, and comfortable. Alone, they were permitted to make out near the rear exit of the restaurant, for more than an hour.

Paradise...

Sheer paradise...

12

Patrick and Billy found Marty's DVDs where they'd been all along, in his bedroom. They placed the movies in a couple of boxes then carried them to the Mexican restaurant. Both boys took their time. Neither could be accused of moving swiftly. Patrick was as slow as a snail, despite getting paid for retrieving the movies.

Kris and Marty were no longer doing the "kissy-face" by the time Patrick and Billy arrived. By now, they stood at the restaurant's front entrance, drinking Cokes and chatting. It was almost four in the afternoon. The rain had stopped, though a harsh wind swift through the streets and corridors of town.

"Took ya long enough," griped Marty, once the two younger boys showed up with the movies.

"It was a long ways," moped Patrick, "and them boxes was heavy!"

"Bullshit," cursed Marty, scrounging through the boxes to make sure all of his movies were there. At first, he hollered that *The Bridge on the River Kwai* and the silent classic *The Cabinet of Doctor Caligari* were missing. He then remembered that a history teacher, Mr. Hoffman, had borrowed them. That was cool. Hoffman was kind of a boring old fart, but remained supportive and caring of Kris and Marty.

Sunlight occasionally peeked through darkened storm clouds as the four boys headed toward a quiet neighborhood, where Kris' Aunt Barbara lived.

Aunt Barbara owned a quaint home with a quaint little lawn, quaint flowers lining a steel fence, and a couple of quaint trees offering shade on quaint summer days. There was a yard swing where folks could talk, or enjoy the simple pleasures of a paperback novel. The one-story house was painted in a bright blue, in a residential area where white paint was more acceptable. On the front door was a wooden sign that read *LOVE AND TOLERANCE ARE LOVED AND TOLERATED HERE.*

The four boys entered a dimly lit living room. The furniture consisted of a bean bag chair, weave recliners and chairs with woven cushions and pillows, and a thick shag carpet. Thin blinds and curtains allowed in scant levels of natural light from outside. The smell of incense candles either gave off a calming, soothing odor, or made people want to vomit. On a compact stereo, *The Carpenters* lamented on rainy days and Mondays. It may have been a Sunday, but still seemed dreary and depressing.

Marty figured that Aunt Barbara was weird. Nice, but weird. If nothing more, she offered him a shoulder to lean on whenever times were tough. Occasionally, her language was bad enough to even make him blush.

Barbara was in her sixties, with salt-and-pepper hair. She wasn't tall, but hardly petite. She split her own firewood, went on long walks and bike rides, and remained healthy. This was in contrast to the booze, drugs, and wild sex of her younger days. Her face was weathered, her expressions cheerful, her eyes soulful and even melancholy. Barbara had her share of difficulty, mostly self-imposed, and had the scars and knowledge to prove it. She wasn't afraid to fight for causes she truly believed in. Late in life, she became a mental health counselor. Semi-retired, she continued to help at-risk teens on a contractual basis. That afternoon, Barbara spent time with an adolescent named Shelby Newton.

Shelby was slight in size and appearance. He was Kris and Marty's age but looked younger. He kept his blonde hair neat, straight, and tidy. He had a pale complexion, stood shorter than Patrick and Billy, and was bone-skinny. He dressed in corduroy shorts, white socks, *Hush Puppies*, and a shamrock green sweater with a turtle sewn at the heart.

Shelby was a jittery sort who constantly fidgeted with his socks, or tugged at the collar of his shirt. He was articulate, intelligent, scholarly, extremely quiet, and shy. He wasn't athletic and handsome like Kris, or scruffy and harder-edged like Marty. He was polite, often to his own detriment, He spoke with a noticeable lisp. He wore long sleeves to conceal the scars on his arms and wrists, obtained in attempts to open his veins and end his life. He recently spent a few days at the state funny farm, the same location featured in Ken Kesey's *One Flew Over the Cuckoo's Nest*.

Shelby was now in rehabilitation, and had a challenging road ahead of him. He was regarded as a wussy, a pussy, a wimp, a pansy, a wallflower, a shrinking violet, and a sissy.

Kris was always nice to Shelby. On the other hand, Marty kind of looked down at him. In Marty's mind, there were gay men, and there were faggots. Shelby was a faggot. And the little faggot refused to defend himself, while endlessly putting up with abuse from bullies. Still, it didn't prevent Marty from going to war with five guys, one afternoon at gym class, in order to uphold Shelby.

Aunt Barbara let out a loud cheer, leaped from her chair, and gave her four newcomers each a hug and a kiss. Meanwhile, Shelby shrunk down in his recliner, fidgeted with his socks, tugged at his collar, and tried to be invisible.

Once Kris got done hugging and kissing Aunt Barbara, he went to address Shelby. "How's life?" he asked, pleasantly.

"All ... all right," stuttered Shelby, his soft voice barely audible.

"It's good to see you," said Kris, calmly placing one hand on Shelby's scrawny shoulder.

"I assume you're here to spend the night," Barbara whispered to Marty. "Or maybe even the week."

"You *ass-umed* right," answered Marty. He owed Barbara a great deal, but was too proud and stubborn to admit it.

"Feel free to take your things in the bedroom at the end of the hallway," said Barbara, pointing. "Guess you won't mind bunking in the same room as Kris."

"You guessed it," said Marty, catching sight of Shelby, who looked tiny and frail within a rather large chair. He grinned, leaned over, and slapped Shelby's knee. "How's she hangin', Shel?" he asked, in a loud, blustery tone. "Gettin' it wet there, bub?"

Shelby's eyes widened. An anxious smile highlighted his face.

"I was wondering if I could excuse you boys for a moment?" asked Barbara. "I need to finish up here with Shelby, then we'll sit down with cups of herbal tea."

"Make it a brewsky and yer on!" snickered Marty, hauling one box of DVDs through the darkened hallway.

"Take the rest of Marty's things on in there," Barbara told Kris. "And then I'd like a word with you."

Kris nodded, followed Marty to his room, then sat the second box of movies on one bed.

Patrick and Billy were more interested in going to a nearby bowling alley with a game arcade in the back. Barbara gave them both a couple of dollars in quarters, and sent them on their way.

Kris quietly headed back toward the living room. Barbara met him half-way. "Yes, ma'am?" he whispered.

"Did he get kicked out *again*?" asked Barbara, her forehead creased in frustration and worry.

Kris mouthed 'yes'.

"Is it bad this time?"

"It's always bad," explained Kris. "This time it's worse. Marty pretty much cleaned Lance's clock, after the jerk said he took his movies to a pawn shop."

"I'm sorry," sighed Barbara, in grudging resignation.

"Marty's taking it pretty hard. But you know Marty. He's playing tough."

"He's trying to play tough."

Kris shrugged his shoulders and nodded in agreement.

"Give me a few more minutes with Shelby," said Barbara, "Then I'll heat up some chicken noodle soup and herbal tea, and we'll sit down to a nice, long talk."

Kris turned and started for the bedroom, when Barbara stopped him. "Yes, ma'am?"

Barbara slapped a small, round object in the palm of Kris' hand. Kris looked to find a red, foil package with the word Trojan in bold lettering.

It was a condom.

"Just in case," said Barbara, with a twinkle in her eyes. "Better for you and Marty to be safe tonight, than sorry..."

<h1 style="text-align:center">13</h1>

Marty situated himself in Kris' bedroom. Later, he sat down with Barbara and Kris at the dining table, where they enjoyed hot cups of tea and bowls of chicken noodle soup.

"I know life hasn't been very easy for you," Barbara said to Marty, resting his hand in hers. "I know you haven't been given a very good shake."

Marty pasted a snotty grin on his face.

"I'm sorry things have been so rough on you," added Barbara. "I hope you know life doesn't always have to be that way."

"I can't see things bein' any different than the way they are now," mumbled Marty. "No better, no worse. Just the way it is. Just life, that's all."

"'Just life'?" asked Barbara.

"Just life," repeated Marty. "Nothin' but a suck-ass cock."

"Honey," said Barbara. "I spent two months living in a *'75 Chevy Nova* with a boyfriend who, when he wasn't screwing me, was screwing me over. I never thought my life would get any better. I got myself into a jam, and saw no way out of it. I figured that, eventually, the cops would find my dead body in that cramped little car... no money, no ID, nothing. I'd be buried in some unmarked grave. My family would have no clues as to my whereabouts, if they hadn't already given up on me. Trust me, Marty. Life will get better."

Marty bit his bottom lip. Somehow, he maintained a stupid grin. It failed to conceal the pain and despair in his eyes, or the high-pitched quiver in his voice. "I can't see it gettin' better. Fuck, man. Ain't seen my old man since he up and ran out on us, ten years ago. Now Mom spreads her fuckin' legs to every son of a bitch Loser of the Month that she brings home from the fuckin' bars. The rest of us gotta put up with the Loser's shit until me or Mark decide we had enough of it. Then we throw the fucker out after beatin' shit outa him. A lotta people don't like me and Kris just...Well, just *because*. A lotta people don't like my family 'cause of my bitch mother, or they hate us on account of how we live, or where we live. Goddamn fuckin' white trash of Oregon."

Marty frowned. He had spilled his life story to crazy Aunt Barbara, like he was in a confessional. Oh well. What the fuck? Barbara heard it all before, and kept it to herself.

"Life ain't nothin' but one big suck-ass cock," continued Marty. "Has been, ever since I can remember. Can't see it gettin' no better. Life ain't nothin' but one big suck-ass cock. A'ways has been, a'ways will be."

"Don't say that, Marty," begged Kris. "Please don't say that."

"You don't see me living in a *Chevy Nova* now," said Barbara. "Do you?"

Marty frowned. "Well... No..."

"Life can get better," said Barbara. "It can, Marty, and it will."

"But how?" cried Marty. "How the fuck will Mom ever pull her head outa her fuckin' ass, get her shit together, and act like a real mom to us? Just when will she get her shit together? If she ever fuckin' will."

"She may never get her shit together," said Barbara, flatly.

"Then what makes you think life can get any better?" argued Marty.

"It's not your job to get your mom's act together," explained Barbara. "Sure, you might help her as much as you can. You can bend over backwards to help her. In the end, the only person to help your mom is herself. Right now, I'm not thinking about your mom. I'm thinking about you."

Marty shook his head, in anger, worry, and denial.

"Things will get better for you," said Barbara, "if only you give yourself permission to make them better."

Marty rolled his eyes back. "Whatever...."

"You're a good person, Marty," said Barbara, "even if you make me wonder." She glanced at Kris. "You make us all wonder."

"What difference does it make?" snapped Marty, like he'd been put on the spot. "Why the fuck should anyone worry themselves over me?"

"Someone out there loves you," said Barbara.

Marty slouched.

"I know life hasn't been easy for you," said Barbara. "You're angry and hurt over it. I can't blame you. I'd be angry and hurt, too."

Marty said nothing, though the wheels in his head were spinning.

"Someday, Marty, someday soon," said Barbara, smiling. "You'll find a small house or an apartment to move into. Maybe you'll be there on your own, or with someone else."

Kris and Marty exchanged glances.

"Perhaps you'll be with that special someone who loves you," Barbara went on. "You'll love them, too. Someone who loves and accepts you for who you are...Marty! *Marty McKenna!* And that special someone won't care about your lifestyle, or your background, or how your parents screwed up so badly, or that you and your brothers basically had to raise yourselves. You'll have a good job, a decent roof over your head, then spend every evening with that special someone, and go to sleep with them every night. Might be, you'll live in a town or a neighborhood where people don't care who you are or what you are, or if it honestly amounts to a fuck!"

Marty giggled. He liked it when Barbara cursed like a sailor, and not make it sound like cursing at all. Just talk, that's all. Just talk.

"Shelby Newton told me how you stuck up for him at school," said Barbara, admirably. "I think Shelby needs someone to look up to. I think that someone is you."

"Shelby Newton needs a backbone," said Marty. "Not to mention, a set o' balls between them scrawny legs. Shelby needs to learn how to fuckin' defend himself. I can't be there for 'em all the time!"

"But you do feel good about upholding Shelby when others didn't," said Barbara. "Right?"

"Someone had to help that sissy out!" shouted Marty. "I couldn't just stand there and watch them jerks beat up on 'em, like that. Somebody had to beat the fuck outa them ass-wipes!"

"And that somebody was you," noted Barbara.

"It just happened to be me," said Marty.

"Oh?" questioned Barbara, skeptically.

"Got my ass thrown outa school for about a week over it," said Marty. "No need to make anything more of it."

"I'm not one to condone fighting," said Barbara. "But I'm glad you went out of your way to defend Shelby. It must have felt good to put those ass-wipes in their place."

"Fuck yeah, it did!" laughed Marty, blushing. "It felt good. Real good!"

"Okay." Barbara cleared her throat. "You say that Shelby needs to learn how to defend himself."

"Yeah," said Marty. "So?"

Barbara looked Marty straight in the eye. "Are you willing to defend and uphold your own life and future?"

14

Corey Phipps... aka *Turtlehead*... wandered the rain-soaked streets of Grangeford.

Turtlehead was a solitary figure. His one and only true friend was Mike Moyers... aka Dirtbag. And at that given moment the Dirtbag was hanging out with his brother Lester. This left Turtlehead with no one to hang out with but himself.

Turtlehead had been the object of ridicule and scorn since he could remember. Beginning at the first grade, he was known as "Turtlehead".

Turtlehead...

Turtlehead...

TURTLEHEAD...

Very few knew who Corey Phipps was. But everyone knew Turtlehead.

He couldn't recall exactly who gave him that hated nickname. All he knew is that it happened sometime around Christmas, when another child referred to him as "Turtlehead". Soon, the entire student body at North Grangeford Elementary called him Turtlehead. Rarely did anyone address the rather awkward, homely boy as Corey Phipps.

Turtlehead... That name stuck...

It was a nickname which the rather awkward, homely boy grew to hate, about as much as he hated his mere existence in the occasionally cold and unfriendly town of Grangeford.

Corey Phipps was kind of slow...learning-disabled is what they said about him. He had difficulty reading even the simplest of texts. Math was worse. Corey barely got past two-plus-two.

And forget about multiplication and division!

Teachers grew rather tired and impatient with the rather awkward, homely, learning-disabled kid. Although educators refrained from using the nickname "Turtlehead", it didn't stop them from calling him "lazy", "stupid", "careless", "unmotivated", "lacking" ...

"Retarded".

The worse Corey did in school, the more he fell behind. He failed the second grade and barely squeaked by the other levels. Generally, Corey passed due to "social advancement", and not upon academic achievement. Teachers were glad to push Corey along. For the exception of the special education staff, most educators avoided him as best they could.

Corey was often placed in the back of the classroom. As long as he kept his mouth shut, he spent days drawing stick figures, picking his nose, looking at the clock, and staring off into space until the final bell rang.

Corey Phipps was unpopular. He was good at getting taunted, beat on, and bullied. His only chums were freaks, geeks, goons, weirdos and oddballs who also traveled through life isolated, abandoned, and alone.

In middle school, Corey befriended Mike Moyers...the Dirtbag. Mike was ragged, filthy, unkempt, unwashed. He came from a home of chronic unemployment, alcoholism, drug abuse, and criminal behavior. Mike changed his hand-me-down clothes on average of once a week. In an impoverished house with several young-uns, there simply wasn't the money for nice duds.

Nobody liked the Moyers. *Nobody!* Still, a few churches tried helping them out with charity and job offers. The Moyers usually screwed things up, by repaying kindness with lawlessness and crass stupidity.

The Dirtbag never stood a chance! The realities of being a lowlife and a thief undermined hopes of ever making something of himself. The Dirtbag settled on being nothing more, or nothing less, than the Dirtbag. He knew his place in the world, and there was little competition.

The Dirtbag and Turtlehead were the lowest of the low. No one ranked lower than that. The world never allowed it! No one could be as lowly, despicable, or disgusting as those two morons.

Even the McKennas weren't that bad, despite their shortcomings and rough edges. Mark had a shitty job. Patrick was fat and never worked at anything...

And Marty? ... Well, Marty was Marty...

A greasy-spoon waiter, a fat-ass, and a homo. And still, they weren't near as bad as the Dirtbag and Turtlehead!

Even a wimpy, whining, prancing little fairy like Shelby Newton wasn't as pathetic! Shelby had potential! He was pleasant, kindhearted, non-threatening, and agreeable. No one at Grangeford High played piano and guitar as well as Shelby! In chorus, his lisping, high-pitched falsetto slowly surrendered to a deeper, more confident singing voice. The speech, drama, and music nerds loved and appreciated Shelby!

The only place for the Dirtbag and Turtlehead was in the gutter. Right in the stinking gutter!

Turtlehead spent a few lonely minutes aimlessly strolling the aisles of the local *Safeway*, looking for nothing in particular. The employees kept a close eye on him, making sure he didn't make a five-finger discount on items.

Turtlehead was no thief. Stealing was the Dirtbag's specialty! Turtlehead was guilty by association. At the moment, he hung around *Safeway* simply to stay out of the wet weather. Once the rain stopped, he again wandered through the cold, breezy streets of town.

Turtlehead lived alone with this mother, who didn't approve of television, the internet, or rock music. There was nothing to do at home but listen to Gospel tunes and Christian radio. Conversation between mother and son consisted of "God this!" or "God that!" or "God loves this!" or "God hates that!" or ....

"God!"

"GOD!"

"GOD!"

As a result, Turtlehead spent time with the Dirtbag, or spent time by himself. He often wandered aimlessly, suffering the evil eye from those who distrusted and loathed him, while also getting insulted, picked on, or beat up.

Getting beat up is exactly what happened to Turtlehead, in front of *McCleary's Bookstore*. One moment, Turtlehead examined a poster for the latest Stephen King thriller. The next moment he heard, "Goddamn motherfuckin' son of a bitch! Gonna kick yer fuckin' ass!"

Turtlehead then saw lightning bolts and stars, as someone struck his now bloody nose.

Turtlehead flew backwards, into the brick wall of the bookstore. Before he knew it, he collapsed into a muddy, rain-soaked sidewalk. One side of his face stung and swollen. His eyesight grew slightly out of focus, while his thoughts clouded. Mouth filled with blood.

Turtlehead knew he'd been hit...but by what?

He soon recognized the angry, hostile voice. Knowing he was under attack, Turtlehead struggled to flee from the danger... if he could. In one corner of his eye, he saw a scruffy figure with long, unruly red hair, dressed in a hoody, cut-offs, and filthy shoes.

McKenna... Marty McKenna...

With Marty was Billy Rodriquez, his fat little brother Patrick...and fuck-buddy Kris.

Marty sent his right foot into Turtlehead's gut. Air rushed from Turtlehead's mouth. Pain engulfed his entire body. He doubled over, as both hands covered his belly. Blood spilled from his nose.

Repeatedly, Marty kicked Turtlehead's shins, thighs and knees, in an attempt to nail his balls. "Get up, y' fuckin' pile o' shit!" he cursed. "Get yer ass up, so I can beat fuck outa you, s'more!"

"Don't!" screamed Kris. "Don't hurt him, Marty! *Please!*"

"I ain't gonna hurt 'em!" Marty shouted back. "I'm gonna kill 'em!"

Billy and Patrick stood back, wondering if stomping Turtlehead would bring them closer to retrieving the video games. They weren't even sure if Turtlehead was a sympathetic character, or a deserving one. Still, it gave Patrick a sense of satisfaction and glee to watch Marty rip Turtlehead a new one.

"Get the fuck up!" commanded Marty, now aiming his attacks on Turtlehead's arms and hands.

"I didn't take them games!" shrieked Turtlehead, his high-pitched voice echoing throughout the steel and concrete canyon of Main Street. "Mike's got 'em, not me!"

"Maybe you ain't got 'em, but you sure the fuck was there when the asshole took 'em!" Marty kicked Turtlehead's spine. "Soon as I'm done with you, I'm goin' after Dirtbag!"

"Stop it!" yelled Kris, angry, upset, and disappointed with Marty... the same Marty he swore to love and uphold. "Stop it, Marty! *Now!*"

"The fuck I'm gonna stop it!" giggled Marty, pressing one foot into Turtlehead's hand. "Now I'm gonna ask if this retard ever picked his feet in Poughkeepsie!"

A split-second later, Kris slapped Marty's smiling face.

Everyone grew deathly quiet. Billy and Patrick both gasped, as their eyes widened in fear and disbelief.

Kris just slapped Marty...

Kris slapped Marty!

Even Kris was shocked. He had slapped Marty...the Marty he loved and cherished more than anyone...the Marty he loved yet never fully understood or condoned. This, despite their commitment and devotion to one another.

Kris had slapped Marty. He now wondered if maybe, just maybe, he went too far. What choice did he have? He had to put a stop to Marty's brutality against Corey Phipps. And the only way to stop the brutality was, in of itself, brutal.

Kris was divided between apologizing to Marty, or standing his ground. The only sounds came from the screeching tires of a dump truck at an intersection, Turtlehead sprawled out on the cold, wet sidewalk, wheezing, whining and bawling, and rain beating against cement and pavement.

Initially, Marty was so blinded by rage that he didn't realize Kris had struck him. Once the truth had entered his chaotic mind, he turned to face the one who betrayed him.

Kris swallowed. He loved Marty, he feared Marty, yet rarely did he "get" Marty. Nor did he tolerate Marty's volatile, unpredictable nature. At the same time, he wondered if he was blowing it with God...the everlasting and loving God in Heaven above. The God who created Kris English, gave him life and the ability to know right from wrong, based upon spiritual ideals and principles. The God who endowed man with free will, along with the drive and desires to grant unwavering faith in Him. The God that some claimed had loved homosexuals, yet condemned homosexuality.

"I didn't take them games!" cried Turtlehead, dragging himself over the muddy sidewalk. "Mike's got 'em, not me!"

"Maybe so," said Marty, kicking Turtlehead's torso, "but you just stood there and let 'em take the fuckin' things."

"Stop it!" begged Kris. "Please Marty. Just stop it!"

"The fuck I'm gonna stop it!" responded Marty. "The fuck d' you expect from me, Kris? Just stand around with my thumb up my ass, lettin' these sorry piles o' shit beat the fuck outa my little brother?" Marty slugged Kris' shoulder. "Fuck's the matter with you? Just what the fuck's the matter with?"

"Stop it!" exploded Kris, tears streaming from his eyes.

Marty grinned. "And just what the fuck're you gonna do about it,

Kristoffer? Hit me again, ya limp-wristed pussy? Hit me again? Go for it. Fuck yeah! Go for it! I can sure as fuck hit a lot harder'n you can! You ever think about hittin' me again, Kris, I'll send you spinnin' into the middle o' next week!"

"One more word out of you," wept Kris, "and it's over between us. We're done!"

Marty glared at Kris.

"Just one more word." Kris turned away from Marty. His frail emotions were devastated. He questioned if he had the means and the courage to fully speak his mind. "One more word, or one more blow against Corey, and we're done." Kris took a deep breath. "I'm breaking up with you, and...and we're *done*."

"Faggots," snickered Patrick.

"Bullshit," cursed Marty. "Bull-fuckin'-shit! Y'ain't breakin' up with me. Y'ain't never gonna break up with me! Ya ever think about breakin' up with me, I'll fuckin' crack yer skull open!" Marty allowed a few tears to slip from his own eyes. "I swear!"

Edith McCleary just stepped from the bookstore which carried her name to find Turtlehead lying on the sidewalk, howling like a hungry infant. Nearby was Kris and Marty, either having a heated exchange or a lovers' quarrel, Yards away were Billy and Patrick, standing around like a couple of silly twerps, doing what silly twerps do best, which was nothing.

Edith was a petite woman, under a bundle of dyed-black hair, and eyes concealed behind thick, wireframed glasses. She was well-respected in the community. She had spent a number of years on the city council, and owned a successful business for more than forty years. She was charitable, and orchestrated a number of fundraisers in and around Grangeford. Despite a lack of height, Edith more than made up for it with an esteemed background and various accomplishments.

This wasn't lost on Kris English. Nor was it lost of Marty McKenna.

A sense of guilt swept over the four boys...most notably Marty. As usual, stubborn pride destroyed any hopes of remorse or reconciliation.

"What's wrong with you, Marty?" scolded Edith, disgusted by the image of Corey crawling like a worm in front of her bookstore. "Just what in the name of God is wrong with you?"

Marty didn't answer. Instead, he looked away from Edith. He slowly, painfully, turned to face Billy, then Patrick - and finally at Kris.

Kris.

Kris and Marty stared at each other. Neither spoke as tears filled their eyes. Both struggled to speak. Words failed them.

"Marty," pleaded Kris, refusing to allow the ties which bound him to his boyfriend to suddenly fray and tear apart. "Mart.... Marty...."

There was no debating Kris and Marty's love for one another. Yes, Kris loved Marty, and he feared him. More than anything, he dreamed of spending the rest of his life with Marty. Was that possible now? No matter how much Kris may have loved Marty, he failed to grasp the anger and rage which constantly seethed within him. Living with Marty would never, could never be easy. Was it worth the strain and effort?

Well, there were always other fish in the sea. Was Kris willing to give up on Marty, and attempt to catch a new one? And would God understand and accept him, if he did?

Kris reached out to caress Marty's face, his vision blurred and clouded by tears.

Marty pulled away from Kris. "Go fuck yerselves!" he cursed at everybody, at nobody, and mainly at *himself*.

Marty spit on Turtlehead, then turned away from the others. With nothing more to say, he walked away from Turtlehead, away from Billy Rodriquez, away from his fat little brother Fatrick... and away from Kris.

Marty evolved into a solitary figure as he slowly disappeared through the fog, haze, and darkness of a wet, dreary night.

15

"Fuck!" shrieked Marty, storming through the side streets and alleys of Grangeford. "Fuck, fuck, fuck, fuck, cocksucker, cunt!"

Marty was pissed. Goddamned pissed. He was pissed because he didn't get to beat up Turtlehead as bad as he wanted to. He was pissed because Kris fucking prevented him from fully stomping a sorry piece of shit. He was pissed because Edith McCleary caught him tromping on Turtlehead and jumped him for it.

Marty was pissed because he demanded an apology from Kris for slapping him...and Kris wouldn't fucking do it. What a bunch of bullshit! What a cowardly bunch of bullshit!

Who was Kris to criticize Marty for anything? Who was the one to help "out" Kris in the first place? Huh? *Huh?* If it wasn't for Marty, Kris would still be in the fucking closet and scared of himself, of who he truly was and scared of people knowing it.

Marty was pissed off because it was easier to be pissed off, rather than to find reasons not to be so pissed off.

Marty was always pissed off. All the time. He couldn't recall a day when he wasn't pissed off about something. He was pissed off at Kris, at his own fucking family, at the Dirtbag and Turtlehead, at Edith McCleary, at growing up in a shithole like Grangeford, at the shitty fucking weather....And at life itself.

Mostly, Marty was pissed off at himself.

Marty was blinded by rage, the same way he was blinded by the fog and the haze, just like he was blinded by the rain and the tears spilling from his eyes.

It embarrassed and humiliated Marty to cry. It was wussy and pussy and wimpy to cry! Crying was for bitches and whiners and wimps like Shelby Newton, but not for Marty McKenna. And yet, a day rarely went by where Marty didn't cry about something. He often cried himself to sleep, and woke up crying. No one knew about it, other than Marty himself along with God in Heaven above.

Marty didn't know why he was pissed off all the time, or why he found himself overwhelmed by sadness, anger, confusion and fear. This was always the way things were since recollection. Marty was constantly mad at the world, mad at life, and mad at every loudmouth son of a bitch who got in his face for being white trash, or the son of a drunken skank, or because he liked guys and not girls, or being mad at himself, or simply being mad *because*.

Marty didn't ask to be white trash, or the son of a skanky drunk ... or gay. He wasn't sure if those issues were truly his fault. Certain assholes believed they were entirely his fault! Just because he was white trash, or the son of a drunken skank, or gay didn't mean he had to cow down to bullshit. It didn't mean he had to be pitiful or pathetic or privileged, or doomed to Hell. He was praised and cursed because he loved Kris, and because Kris loved him.

He was also praised and cursed for defending Shelby Newton.

Marty got invited to some goddamn pride parade bullshit up in Portland, simply because he liked guys and not girls. He refused because he didn't care to be praised or cursed or damned and demeaned or placed on a fucking pedestal simply because of who he was and what he was. Fuck if he was going to march up and down the streets of Stumpville, carrying fucking pride flags and wearing a stupid-assed shirt reading *KISS ME, I'M GAY*, or any other faggot shit. He was a human, not a statistic or a stereotype or image of what others expected him to be.

He was nobody but Marty...Marty McKenna. He wanted to be loved or hated or accepted or rejected for who he was and what he was...Marty McKenna, and nobody else. He simply wanted to live his own life as a human being, and as a person, and as a man, no better or no worse or any different than anyone else! Or if people loved him or hated him, merely for loving Kris English.

More than anything, Marty wanted to be treated like a kid and left the fuck alone!

Marty sat on a rail of an abandoned railroad track. His head was cluttered and chaotic with thoughts sprinting through his mind like lightning, at odds with themselves.

Fuck, man.

Marty stared into the darkness, at a distant intersection. Cars travelled here and there, taking passengers to night jobs, home, on visits, to the movies, or wherever the hell they were going. Marty cinched up the hood of his sweatshirt. His bare legs remained exposed to the weather, but who cared?

Marty quietly watched the seemingly endless stream of cars, hauling their passengers *somewhere.* Little by little, he wondered if he was on a downward spiral, heading deeper and deeper into an abyss, leading him nowhere.

Part of Marty said fuck Kris English, fuck the Dirtbag, fuck Turtlehead, fuck Fatrick McKenna, fuck Billy Rodriquez and his fucking video games, fuck Edith McCleary, fuck Grangeford, and fuck everybody and everyone and everything under the delusion that life was grand.

It wasn't.

No matter. Marty couldn't forget what Aunt Barbara told him over hot cups of tea and bowls of hot chicken noodle soup. Things will get better, if only he gave them permission to be so.

Marty wanted to believe that, if only he gave himself permission to accept it. If only he gave himself permission to work for it. If only he gave himself permission to fight for his mere existence, his own life, his potential, and his future. Or was it easier to just say "fuck it", which he'd been doing forever? Was it easier to stomp around town in a hoody, his cut-off jeans, his ugly Adidas, and then fight every son of a bitch who crossed him, rather than to fight for something better?

Was it easier just to stay pissed?

Marty was also unable to forgo what Barbara said about a "special someone" to own a home with, enjoy dinner with every night, share a bed and make love with, and have a life together. A special someone who loved Marty, simply for being Marty, A special someone... someone like Kris English?

If Kris was Marty's "special someone", did that also mean that Marty was Kris' "special someone" too?

Fuck, man...

Marty had to find Kris, apologize for being a dickwad and an ass-lick, then apologize for tromping Turtlehead (although he was far from feeling sorry over it!) and then maybe, just maybe, apologize for being Marty... no matter how much Kris loved him! Would Marty give himself permission to apologize and admit that he was wrong, and have the courage to say "I'm sorry" or have an ability to say "I love you"?

"I love you".

Fuck, man.

Marty was always pissed off, even when he wasn't. He couldn't imagine not being pissed off. Pissed off was normal, as normal as eating, breathing, sleeping, laughing, pulling his pud, or merely getting by. Would he give himself permission not to be pissed off?

Marty hated being pissed off. He also relished it. Being pissed off gave him the right to be pissed off, to stomp around town saying "fuck this" and "fuck that" and "fuck you" and "fuck off" or assuming a "fuck it" attitude about it all.

Marty denied happiness. He never believed in happiness, and never trusted it. Happiness was an illusion, something which either escaped or eluded him. Happiness was temporary. Anger was constant.

Anger was his friend. It was also an enemy.

Life was nothing but one big suck-ass cock. Life had given Marty an endless supply of shit sandwiches, to go along with the cheap-ass, dollar store ramen, mac and cheese, oatmeal and dried beans tucked away in the pantry.

Life wasn't the only thing which gave Marty shit sandwiches. More often than not, he gave them to himself. He gagged shit sandwiches down each and every morning, claiming to be repulsed when, in truth, he savored them. He gained strength from shit sandwiches, and grew tough from such a disgusting diet.

Anger defined Marty McKenna. It was the reason he fought in order to defend Kris or little Shelby Faggot Newton or Fatrick or Billy Rodriquez.... or fucking video games. It also moved him to help out nice people like Barry and Abigail Thatcher. Anger pushed him to do the right thing, and offer them a needed hand. It also motivated him to beat up E or that sorry pile of shit, Loser of the Month Lance.

Marty wondered now if anger might get him thrown in prison, or lead to an early grave.

What did Marty love more...anger or Kris English? Was he willing to fight for the ability to stay angry all the time? Or was he willing to fight for something much more rewarding, and far more difficult, such as happiness?

Fuck, man.

Guilt and shame assaulted Marty McKenna. Stubborn pride and anger surrendered to sadness and sorrow. Uncertainty and doubt were in charge. This left Marty weak and vulnerable, an empty shell of himself.

Marty not only lacked answers, but even the means to find them.

Marty pressed his face to his bare legs and knees, then released a high-pitched wail. He cried like never before. He cried for things he'd been screwed out of. He cried for those who truly mattered, such as Mark and Patrick. He cried for far-reaching and challenging goals. He wept for that which always avoided him the most...*Happiness.*

More than anything, Marty cried for the happiness, security, and peace of mind he hoped to find with Kris English...A peace of mind he feared never to possess...A peace of mind he refused to go after.

Anger was easy, man. Too fucking easy.

Marty now bawled his eyes out, like a wimp and a whiner and a bitch and a wussy and a pussy and a sissy. He bawled even louder than Shelby Newton when he got bullied in gym class, before Marty stepped in and beat the fuck out of those five cocky assholes. He bawled for the father who ran out on him and his two brothers, years before. He bawled for the mom who loved the booze and the weed and the Losers of the Month more than she did her own kids. He bawled for the boy who loved him more than anything, the boy who loved him more than life itself, the boy who loved him for being nothing more or nothing less than just being Marty...Marty McKenna.

Fuck, man...*Oh fuck, man!*

You're actin' like a pussy...a wimpy, whiny, fuckin' pussy!

Goddamn it, Marty! ...Grow the fuck up and act like a fuckin' man for once in yer life! *Fucker!*

Asshole motherfucker!

Marty slapped himself across the face, as hard as he could. He didn't know why, he just did.

And then he did it again...

And again...

And again... And again...

And again, and again, and again... Until he heard someone speak up in the darkness and say, "The fuck's wrong with you, homo?"

16

Startled, Marty looked up to see one of the lowlifes he spent all day searching for...one of the lowlifes he kicked shit out of earlier...a lowlife who needed to get the shit kicked out of, once more.

Mike Moyers... aka the Dirtbag. The asshole fucking Dirtbag.

And now the Dirtbag caught Marty carrying on like a whiny, wimpy, wussy, pussy little bitch.

Marty gasped.

Normally, it never frightened Marty to see the Dirtbag. Normally, the Dirtbag was frightened of him. Normally, the Dirtbag would make some rude fucking comment about Marty's homo-tude, as a means of concealing the fact that he was shitting his pants prior to getting the shit kicked out of him.

Normally, Marty would out-cuss, out-insult, and outsmart the Dirtbag, to the point where the Dirtbag would swing at him, just to find himself on the ground, screaming and hollering and carrying on like he was on the verge of dying.

Normally, Marty never whined or whimpered or moped or cried or carried on like a crybaby little bitch. And now the Dirtbag... the piece of shit Dirtbag, caught Marty carrying on like a crybaby little bitch!

Fuck, man.

Marty felt like a fool, an idiot, a numbskull, a moron, a half-wit, a douchebag, in front of the worst person on the entire planet....

The Dirtbag.

The Dirtbag smiled. It pleased him to see Marty carrying on like a crybaby little bitch. He had no clue what the faggot was crying about. He had every intention of using it against him come September, once school started. Everyone at the high school knew Marty was queer. And now he was even acting like it! Wonderful! Abso-fucking-lutely wonderful!

Maybe Marty and his bed-buddy Kris got into a spat. And now Kris was taking it up the ass for someone else.... Shelby Newton, maybe. And now poor little faggot Marty was all alone in the world, left with no one to love, or slap the shit out of during a lovers' quarrel. Therefore, he was left with no one else to slap but himself. Just like the wussy, pussy little fag he truly was.

And now it was Marty's turn to crawl.

"Kris finally had enough o' yer shit, Queer-Boy?" laughed the Dirtbag, thinking that once, just this once, he had the upper hand over Marty McKenna.

Frantically, Marty struggled to wipe away the snot and tears and somehow regain his composure, then become the man he so wished to be... before kicking the Dirtbag's ass.

"Hit him, Mike!" someone shouted from behind.

Fuck, man. Oh fuck, man!

Turtlehead!

Marty hopped to his feet. He had already stomped the Dirtbag and Turtlehead earlier that day, and required little effort in taking them on at the same time. He was now forced into kicking both of their asses to keep them from spouting off for catching him crying and carrying on like a crybaby little bitch.

The problem was, Marty no longer wanted to kick their asses. He'd done so already, on several occasions. All he wanted now was to get Billy's games back, or stomp the Dirtbag and Turtlehead if they failed to comply. More than anything, Marty simply wanted to get the games back like a good little son of a bitch, then return to Kris' good graces...show his love and affection for Kris, the best way he knew how, then vow to remain with Kris 'til the end of time, and somehow make an honest, heartfelt commitment.

"Figured you had to bring your toady along to watch me hurt you?" Marty growled at the Dirtbag. "Never knew you was that eager for an audience."

The Dirtbag took a step back. He was there to do what he'd been wanting to do for the longest time, which was to clean Marty's clock. "I...I come to settle scores," he stuttered, unable to conceal fear for confronting a homo who, just moments before, was crying his eyes out for losing his bed-buddy to another homo. "Gonna... gonna make you wish you'd never been born, McKenna!"

"And you need Turtlehead's help for that?" laughed Marty. Desires to start over suddenly gave way to teaching the Dirtbag yet another lesson, before beating up Turtlehead again. "Two against one's nigger fun. Don't look like you two niggers are up to it."

"Heard you been lookin' for me all day," said the Dirtbag. "Here I am. Fuck do ya want from me?"

"You beat the hell outa my little brother," said Marty, "then swiped Billy Rodriquez' games. You gimme them games back, then get yer ugly-ass face outa my life, and we'll all walk away from here, alive an' happy."

"Only reason I beat Pat up was for getting back at you for what you done to me earlier!" the Dirtbag shrieked, fear revealing itself in his quivering voice.

Marty frowned. He now felt somewhat at fault for what happened to Patrick. Still, he refused to admit it. "You beat up my brother for what I done?" he commented. "Pretty bad when a sorry piece o' shit like you can't even beat up a sissy little faggot like me. So whadda ya do? Take it out on some fat, lazy-ass kid instead." Marty turned to face Turtlehead. "Pretty bad when you gotta bring this retard along to watch me kick shit outa you."

"Go fuck yourself!" the Dirtbag screamed. "I'll get them games back to ya. Got 'em in that same fuckin' box I...I found 'em in. Why the fuck would I want 'em? Shit, I ain't even got a TV or nothin' to play 'em on. I..." The Dirtbag swallowed. "I'll get 'em back to ya, so just shut yer ass up and... and... and fuck yourself!"

"Fuck myself?" Marty laughed. "Don't know how. Maybe you oughta drop yer pants, shove yer cock straight up yer filthy, stinkin' ass, and show me how it's done."

Believing he had the Dirtbag over a barrel, Marty began to hum *Garry Owen*. The Dirtbag would hand over them fucking games over to him, then walk away like the chickenshit coward he was, and always would be.

The last thing Marty expected was for Turtlehead to whack him over the head with an eighteen-inch long, plastic conduit, tucked away in his jacket.

Turtlehead's first blow did little damage, thanks to the hood of Marty's sweatshirt. The attack was awkward and clumsy. For the most part, it merely brushed one corner of Marty's noggin.

Marty snickered just as Turtlehead struck him again...this time in the face.

Marty dropped to his knees, in shock and disbelief. His entire body felt weak and wobbly. Initially, the force of Turtlehead's blow was followed by a strange, numbing sensation. The pain then grew steadily worse, as it spread across his cheek and jaw. Tears seeped from both eyes, as thoughts got muddled and cloudy. Marty knew what Turtlehead did to him. He simply didn't believe it. He simply couldn't fucking believe it!

Marty let out a sly, self-deprecating chuckle which soon evolved into a loud, ear-splitting scream. For several seconds, he feared passing out. Somehow, he maintained consciousness. He reached up to run his fingers across his swollen face, wondering if Turtlehead had done permanent damage, or if it'd leave him forever mangled and homely.

Good thing he was Scots and Irish. Otherwise, that fucking retard might have killed him!

Turtlehead's assault was only the beginning, as the Dirtbag slammed his foot squarely into Marty's head.

Marty flew backward. He opened his mouth to issue a volley of insults and cusswords. Instead, blood exploded from his mouth.

Repeatedly, the Dirtbag kicked Marty in the chest, the ass, and the belly. And if that wasn't bad enough, Turtlehead took this opportunity to join in.

Marty rolled himself in a ball, struggling to protect his ribs, stomach, and balls from the onslaught. No good. Usually, the Dirtbag and Turtlehead were loud talk, wussies, pussies, and pansies. Unfortunately, those two loud-talking wussies, pussies, and pansies had gotten the better of Marty.

As two ass-licks took turns on him, the rain got heavier and heavier, until it was a downpour.

Marty lay in loose pebbles dnd gravel, next to a couple of abandoned railroad tracks. He was soaked, drenched, and filthy. Sharp stones cut into his bare legs, found themselves into his clothing, and made an already bad evening into a horrible one.

This wasn't the first time Marty faced humiliating defeat. It was simply the harshest. It was bad enough, getting his ass kicked. It was unbearable, knowing he was getting his ass kicked by the lowest of the low. Those scumbags fought like bitches and fairies. No matter. It still hurt like a dirty son of a bitch!

Marty's thoughts got more fuzzy, foggy, confused and disoriented. The pissing weather only added to a nightmare which he feared never to live down. No matter. Marty swore to get even with those two shitwads, even if it meant digging two unmarked graves in a high-mountain desert south of Grangeford. "Stop it!" screeched Marty, as the Dirtbag planted a foot into his kidneys. "Stop fuckin' hurtin' me, ya goddamn, mother-fuckin' twat face!"

"'Twat face'?" the Dirtbag shouted, kicking Marty's kneecaps. "I'll make you think 'twat face', ya mouthy little prick!"

"Stop it, stop it, *stop it!*" begged Marty, his shrill voice competing with the howls of an oncoming train. "Stop fuckin' kickin' me, ya cheap-ass whores!"

"I'll stop, awright," said the Dirtbag, spitting in Marty's face, "when I'm damn good and ready to!"

"I'm sorry!" bawled Marty. "Just stop fuckin' kickin' me, and I prom-ise.... I promise, never to bother you again!" Tears rolled down Marty's cheeks, mixed with mud, blood, rain, and Dirtbag spit. "I'm done, I'm over, I'm through! Ya whipped my ass good, Dirtbag. Ya ... ya whipped me!"

"You sure about that?" asked the Dirtbag.

"I'm sure!" whimpered Marty, revealing sadness and regrets not only for all the rotten things he'd done in life, but for the rotten things he now planned to do, in retaliation. "I swear it, Dirtbag!"

"*What?*"

"*Mike!*" sobbed Marty, desperately. "Mike... Michael... Mr. Moyers ... *Sir!*"

The Dirtbag smiled victoriously as he shot a glance at Turtlehead.

"I'm sorry," mumbled Marty. "Sorry for all the shitty things I done to ya..."

(*Asshole...*)

(*Let's see how fuckin' sorry you are after I kick your balls loose...*)

Tears streamed from Marty's eyes. Snot seeped from his nose, as blood drooled down his chin. "Just lemme go, Mr. Mike! Just lemme go, and I promise never t' bother you again!"

"I know you won't," laughed the Dirtbag, trading self-satisfactory smiles with Turtlehead. "I don't wanna see you around, McKenna! Don't wanna see either you or your bed-buddy! Got it?"

Marty looked up at the Dirtbag, his vision blurred by rain and tears. "Nothin' t' worry about," he whispered, slithering on the ground between the Dirtbag and Turtlehead like a worm. "Y'ain't gonna have t' deal with me, no more."

"Good deal," sighed the Dirtbag. "'Cause if I ever do see you again, I'm gonna have to beat your cock-lickin' ass."

"Just one more thing," said Marty, giving the Dirtbag a defiant grin.

The Dirtbag rolled his eyes back. "*What?*"

Marty latched onto a stone, large enough to fill his entire hand, and slammed it into the Dirtbag's right foot.

At first, the Dirtbag did nothing but stare at Marty in disbelief. His grin was swiftly replaced with expressions of horror. As his eyes bugged out, he let out a wild, hair-raising shriek.

Marty then sent the stone into the Dirtbag's crotch. Air rushed out of the Dirtbag's mouth, as he bent over and dropped to the ground.

Turtlehead stood to one side, witnessing this event. His thoughts initially registered disconnect. He was under the impression that the Dirtbag had control of the situation. They had beaten hell out of Marty McKenna, and put the sawed-off fairy in his place.

How could that same sawed-off fairy suddenly gain control over the Dirtbag?

The Dirtbag rolled around on the gravel, fighting to catch a breath as both hands clutched his aching scrotum. A bizarre, warped sense of humor entered Turtlehead's mind. The Dirtbag was his one and only friend. It was oddly comical that his one and only friend was now in pain, misery, agony, and torture. Turtlehead was unsure whether to stand back, come to the Dirtbag's rescue, or strike against Marty.

Marty slowly got to his feet and, fighting to maintain his balance, faced Turtlehead. "Motherfucker," he cursed, revealing bloodstained teeth in a lobsided grin. "Yer turn, motherfucker..."

In response, Turtlehead swung the plastic conduit at Marty's head.

Marty blocked Turtlehead's arm with one hand. A split-second later, he sent a right uppercut into Turtlehead's nose. Turtlehead dropped the conduit and staggered backwards, *Sam Peckinpah* style. He tripped over a steel railing on the train tracks and landed hard, across the decaying boards. Marty leaned over Turtlehead and sent two clenched fists into his face and stomach, over and over and over again.

Turtlehead cried out for Marty to halt his aggression against him. No good. Marty literally jumped into Turtlehead with both hands, both feet, both knees and both elbows.

Rain mixed with blood as Marty took his anger, hurt, rage and frustration out on Turtlehead. He didn't care if it was Turtlehead he pounded, or the Loser of the Month, or his mother E, or an absent father, or *himself*. He let it all out. It was Turtlehead who took the blunt of it.

It was Marty who shed the most tears.

Reality and existence were nothing but one big suck-ass cock. Marty battled to get back at all the bullshit he was forced to endure... living in a shitty trailer, on a shitty street, in a shitty neighborhood, in a shitty small town. He didn't ask for the absent father, the drunken, drugged-out mom, the asshole Losers of the Month...none of it! It was his lot in life, and he resented hell out of it!

Was there anything in this life that Marty McKenna didn't resent?

"Back off, McKenna," a low, gruff voice spoke in the darkness. "Unless you want another mouth running across your scrawny neck..."

17

Marty froze as he felt the smooth, shiny, sharpened blade of a hunting knife pressed against his throat. He gazed upon the cuffs of a plaid, long-sleeved shirt, along with a hairy, meaty paw.

Meanwhile, someone breathed hot air down his neck.

Marty's rage was replaced by shame and guilt.

Lester Moyers... the only member of the Dirtbag clan who made something of himself and didn't become a Dirtbag like the rest.

"Mind telling me what's going on?" demanded Lester. His tone was calm, yet carried hints of threat and menace.

Marty didn't answer. How could he? How could he possibly explain that this useless conflict was over nothing more than stupid video games? "Dirtbag," Marty started to say, then quickly changed it to, "Mike.... Yer brother Mike...Mike beat up my brother Pat, then stole Billy Rodriquez' games."

"The fuck we stole 'em!" argued the Dirtbag. "We was... we was gonna give 'em back! We was just tryna get back against Marty for what he done to us!"

"What did you do to Mike and Corey?" Lester questioned Marty.

"Give 'em a hard time," answered Marty. "That's all."

"Is that *all?*" asked Lester, sarcastically.

"It wasn't my idea for them to go after Pat and Billy," explained Marty, "for what *I* done."

Lester released Marty, folded up the knife, and slipped it back into his pocket. "When did they beat on Patrick?" he asked.

"This morning," said Marty, turning to eye the darkened silhouette of Lester Moyers.

Lester was a brawny young man who lifted weights, and had the physique to prove it. He wasn't a bad-looking fella, but showed the same rough, pock-marked cheeks he shared with his old man and brother Mike. The fact that Lester had a decent job, was buying a house, and wore nice clothes separated him from his kin. He carried himself with a pride that his family would never, could never convey.

Marty respected Lester and kind of idolized him, the same way he respected and idolized Edith McCleary. Lester had done very well for himself. Because of it, Marty hoped to step away from a fucked-up life and become a better man. "Sorry, man," he apologized, wiping away the mud, blood and tears from his face. "Real sorry, Lester, for what *I* done."

"Fuckin' faggot," the Dirtbag snarled, painfully hobbling toward Lester's red *Toyota Tacoma.* "Gonna kick your ass when you're least expectin' it."

"'That'll be the day'," said Marty, again trying to sound like John Wayne in *The Searchers.*

"You got Billy's games?" Lester asked the Dirtbag.

"Hell yeah, we got 'em!" shouted the Dirtbag. He leaned against the Toyota to remove one shoe and examine his injured foot.

"Well?" asked Lester. "Where are they?"

Turtlehead staggered across the railroad tracks, reached under a rusted, abandoned *Studebaker* truck, and fetched the box with Billy's games. He dropped the box at Marty's feet, and went to join the Dirtbag.

"Get in the rig," Lester ordered the Dirtbag and Turtlehead. "I've got a few words with McKenna, then I'll take you both home."

The Dirtbag and Turtlehead did as they were told.

"I know what my brother is," Lester said to Marty. "I know he's no good. But he is my brother, and you're not."

"Okay," muttered Marty, cautiously.

"I know you don't like Mike," said Lester, flatly. "Just like I know you got no use for my family. But they're my family. And if I hear about you giving my family any guff, I doubt if they'll locate what's left of your body once I'm through with you."

Marty nodded 'yes'.

Lester opened the car door, gave Marty one last look, and said, "Don't you ever set foot on Dad's property again. I don't care what you think of him. He's my dad. You got that? *My* dad. And I've got more use for him than I ever will for you, Marty McKenna."

Lester got in the Toyota, slammed the door, started the ignition, and drove away.

Marty took a deep breath, retrieved the box with Billy's games, then began his long, wet, arduous journey to Aunt Barbara's. There, he hoped to reaffirm his love and affection to his best friend and dearest companion, Kris English.

If it wasn't too late.

18

"Marty McKenna, you're soaking wet and freezing!"

Once Lester Moyers left with the Dirtbag and Turtlehead, Marty headed toward Aunt Barbara's, a mile or more from the railroad tracks. The rain now came down in buckets, as a cold wind swept in from the northwest. Marty was smeared in mud, blood, snot, sweat and tears. His hoody, cut-offs, and shoes were drenched.

Marty soon experienced the surreal, suffering effects of a fever. His bare legs were black and blue. Blood leaked from his scraped knees, the nose, and the mouth. His face was red and swollen. He had a severe limp, which slowly worsened with every step. Despite it all, Marty smiled happily. He had managed to get Billy's stupid-ass games from a moronic thief and dimwitted pal.

Marty stepped under the eve of a county library, put a cigarette in his mouth, and lit up. His teeth chattered, and both hands shook. He remained exposed to the wind and rain. Sure, he had the shit beat out of him, all right. His one pleasure came from knowing that his adversaries looked and felt a damned sight worse!

Marty's ears burned from the cussing he was undoubtedly getting from the Dirtbag and Turtlehead. Who cared? Who the fuck cared? Marty never liked those piles of shit, anyway. He never liked them, they never liked him, so there. Big fucking deal.

Marty took a drag. He vowed never to get into a brawl with those two piles of shit, ever again. Somehow, he'd gotten the better of them, and they'd hate his guts over it... Forever and forever and forever. Well, fuck 'em, anyway! They were surely going to prison in a few years. Did it matter whether they hated him or not? Eventually, those two failures would be too busy getting screwed by some lifer in the hoosegow, to know or even care what was to become of Marty McKenna. Marty only hoped he wouldn't find himself in there with him, running his ass off to avoid a screwing from the same disgusting, greasy lifer. If Marty was gonna get screwed, he wanted to have a say in the matter!

Some people figured that queers didn't care who screwed them, as long as they were getting screwed. Bullshit. When Marty experienced his first time, he hoped it was with someone he really loved and cherished...

Someone like Kris English.

That asshole Lance, the Loser of the Month, also placed Marty at the top of a shit list. Marty laughed. He'd gotten the best of that fucker, too! It gave him tremendous pleasure, beating that asshole with a fucking trash can. Marty only hoped that E or someone else hadn't called the cops on him for that shit. Lance had it coming, and Marty had the enjoyment of delivering the goods on a worthless son of a bitch.

Even then, the day wasn't without its drawbacks or costs.

It devastated Marty thinking about the look on E's face as they got into it in the back of that shithole tavern. That's the way it always was between E and Marty. They'd start out on speaking terms, move ahead to cussing and screaming, then end up slapping, hitting, and kicking. Then Marty would have to drag his sorry ass to Aunt Barbara's, until the eventual reconciliation, false hopes and promises, and declarations to get off the booze and drugs.

A vicious, endless cycle...

A goddamn vicious, endless cycle...

Marty quietly hummed *Bread of Heaven* and wondered if E would ever free herself from addiction, act like a decent human being, then get a fucking job. Would Marty ever get his shit together, stop getting into fights, develop realistic plans and goals for his life, then make a commitment to Kris?

Fuck, man.

Marty took a last puff from his cigarette, flipped it into the rain, and sighed. He'd head on over to Aunt Barbara's for a few days... and then what? Would he dare? ... could he dare? ... go back home and live with E and whatever Loser of the Month she let in? Lance wasn't the only Loser of the Month that got the shit kicked out of him by Marty. Would that vicious cycle continue? Or was Marty forced to find something new, substantial, long-lasting, and happy?

Was Marty ready to commit himself to Kris or, for that matter, make his own way through life by forever leaving that drafty, leaky old trailer? He was still a kid! Sure, he had a job washing dishes, sweeping the floor, and cleaning the shitters at the *OK Corral.* It wasn't enough to survive on!

And what about that "special someone"? Could Kris and Marty possibly find a place together, then somehow scrape by on whatever jobs they'd find in town - be it at a diner, or pumping gas, or selling candy bars, soda pop, and tater chips at the convenience store?

Fear, panic, and hopelessness swept over Marty McKenna. Fuck! Where could he go from there? Did he truly have a future? If so, would it be with that "special someone"? Someone like Kris? What if Kris really did break-up with Marty, and was no longer that "special someone"?

Fuck, man... Oh fuck, man...

Guilt, shame, and humiliation... along with being soaking wet, battered and bruised, and chilled to the bone.

Fuck!

Marty had no choice but to head to Aunt Barbara's, where a cup of herbal tea, a bowl of chicken noodle soup, and a stern lecture awaited him.

Marty lugged the box filled with the video games and player in the wet weather. The box seemingly grew heavier and heavier with each step. Exhaustion, rain, and a fever nearly got the best of him. What was generally a leisurely walk evolved into a tremendous burden, so much so that Marty nearly left the box on the sidewalk, at the mercy of the rain or whoever happened to find them. Marty's fever almost motivated him to find a nice, soft spot to lie down to take a nap. How grand it'd be to take a needed respite from all of his worries and troubles in the world, curl up in a ball... and die.

"Bread of Heaven, Bread of Heaven... Feed me till I want no more... Feed me till I want no more!"

Once Marty got to Aunt Barbara's, the only one he found there was Kris' sister, Jennifer. She relaxed on a beanbag chair, listening to Barbara's "hippy CDs", this time *Peter, Paul and Mary,* while reading a stupid-assed romance novel. She took a drag from her cigarette and sipped from a bottle of *Black Butte Porter.*

Marty went inside. Blood, rainwater, snot, drool, sweat, and tears dripped onto the carpet. Fever had overtaken him, and he was delirious. He gawked at Jennifer, gave her a lopsided grin, and mumbled, "How she hangin', Li'l Big Sis?"

Jennifer gasped as he spied upon the beaten figure in a hoody and cut-offs. She's seen Marty in various levels of dishevelment, but never like this!

Silence wedged Marty and Jennifer.

Finally, Jennifer dropped the paperback to the floor, lifted herself from the beanbag chair, and cried, "Marty McKenna, you're soaking wet and freezing!"

"Y' think?" commented Marty.

Jennifer pulled the hoody from Marty's torso. She led him to a weave chair, sat him down, and literally yanked his socks and shoes off. "Marty!" she scolded. "Where have you been, and what have you been doing?"

"What was I doin'?" questioned Marty. "What're *you* doin'? Stealing my virginity away from me? Goddamn it, I was savin' myself for Li'l Big Brother, Kristoffer!"

Jennifer dragged Marty through the hallway, to the bathroom. "Take your pants off!" she demanded.

"*Here? Now?*"

"Take a shower!" ordered Jennifer, all loud, mean, and fierce. "Soon as you're done, I want to have a look at you."

"Ain't you seen enough a'ready?" cried Marty.

"Looks like you've been hit by a semi, then dragged through the sagebrush and cactus. Have you been fighting, Marty?"

"Settling scores."

"With that ugly Turtlehead character and stupid Moyers kid?"

"*Bing, bing, bing, bing, bing!*" laughed Marty. "Congratulations! You win the cookie, along with a round trip ticket to *Oz!*"

"Did you get Billy's games back?"

"They're on the porch," answered Marty. "Where's Crazy Aunt Barbara?"

"She took Billy, Pat, and Kris to *McDonalds.*"

"And I don't get done?" moped Marty. "Goddamn fuckin' figures."

"Take a shower, and then we need to talk."

"What am I s'posed to be doin' while we have this *talk*? Sit around, bare-ass naked, while you bitch me out?"

"Kris picked up some clothes from your place. I'll sit them on the counter, next to the sink." Jennifer examined Marty. "Who else survived, *hmm?* Want to tell me that?"

"I won," stated Marty. "You oughta see the losers."

"Are they still alive?"

"They shouldn't be."

Jennifer slapped Marty's backside. "Take a shower," she said. "Get dressed. Then I'll nurse your wounds while we talk."

"Yes, Mom," said Marty, closing the door to clean up.

Slowly, painfully, Marty removed his cut-offs and briefs, which seemingly glued to him from shrinkage and moisture. Carelessly, he tossed them in one corner of the room. He reached into the shower, got the hot water going, then stared at his nude image in a full-length mirror.

No doubt about it. Marty looked like hell. Nearly every inch of his body revealed signs of his fight with the Dirtbag and Turtlehead. Marty knew he deserved every scraped joint, every broken bone and twisted cartilage, every torn and pulled muscle... except where Turtlehead whacked him with that fucking conduit. What bullshit! The worst fucking bullshit imaginable! Retard son of a bitch! Shoulda shoved that conduit up Turtlehead's ass, broke it, then skull-fucked the asshole!

Then again, who'd wanna skull-fuck *that* asshole?

The nastiest wounds Marty suffered was a big-assed bruise under his left arm, and an even nastier one on the right cheek of his scrawny, white, Scots-Irish butt.

Marty frowned. He resembled something that dropped out of the ass of the tallest fucking cow in eastern Oregon. Meanwhile, his pecker had never been so shriveled up since he was five years old.

Marty chuckled at his own expense, then went to take a long, refreshing shower.

Once he finished, Marty located some clean clothes on the counter... a pair of briefs, gym shorts, a long-sleeved Grangeford High tee-shirt, and ankle socks. He quickly dressed, then went to "hear all about it" from Li'l Big Sis, Jennifer. His fever had lifted, as a surge of energy spread throughout his entire body.

Marty sat at a wicker couch. Jennifer handed him a smoke and a bottle of *Henry Weinhard's Private Reserve*, then helped herself to the same. Marty enjoyed the cigarette and the brew, as Jennifer nursed his bare legs with *Neosporin* and salve. He kicked back and kept his mouth shut, although it hurt like hell to have glob smeared all over his injuries.

"You have absolutely no idea how much Kris loves you," said Jennifer.

"What makes ya think I don't know?" argued Marty.

Jennifer sighed. "I dunno, Marty. I just dunno. Maybe you simply don't deserve Kris. Maybe he's too good for you."

Marty pretended like Jennifer's words didn't upset him. He was unable to conceal the pained expressions in his eyes. "Whether I deserve 'em or not," he said, "I love Kris very much. I love 'em in ways you can't even begin to imagine!"

Jennifer grinned, maliciously. "I asked Kris, and he says you two haven't done 'it' yet."

"What about you and my brother Mark?" retorted Marty. "You two done 'it' yet? And what makes ya so sure you deserve Mark? Or if he deserves *you*?"

Jennifer slapped a severe bruise on Marty's upper thigh.

"*Hey!*" cried Marty. "What the motherfuck?"

"I love Kris in ways you can't even begin to imagine, Marty McKenna!" shouted Jennifer. "I can't stand the way you treat him!"

"Whadda ya mean?"

"Telling Billy and Patrick that you guys supposedly fucked in the cemetery, or asking Kris to drop his drawers and bang him in the alley! Do you think that's funny, Marty? Are you really that sick, or just starved for attention?"

"I love Kris, awright?" whined Marty. "*Awright?* I love 'em, goddamn it!"

"You have childish ways of saying it," commented Jennifer.

Marty choked up.

Jennifer sat next to Marty on the wicker couch, and placed her arm around his shoulder. He attempted to refuse her advice and affections. No good. Jennifer squeezed him, in a hug. "Please listen to me, Marty," she spoke, maternally. "I love you as a friend. I love you because you're Mark's brother. I love you because you're Marty. I'm just not sure if I approve of you and Kris being together, or even staying together."

"What do you expect me to do to show how much I love Kris?" whimpered Marty. "What the fuck can I do to prove it?"

"Kris is struggling. He's struggling with his attraction to men, along with his love and concern for you. Part of him still believes that his sexuality is wrong, that it's a sin."

"How is it a sin, if two guys love each other that much?"

"He's worried sick about you," said Jennifer. "He worries that you're going to get into a fight, then get yourself hurt, killed, or thrown in prison. It'd destroy Mark if something terrible happened to you. You're not just Mark's brother. You're his best friend! He thinks he has to stay in Grangeford to look after you and Patrick, even if it means not looking after himself. Do you think it's fair to put him and the rest of us through that?"

Marty said nothing. He simply stared across the room, at the painted flowers and warm blue colors of Aunt Barbara's living room walls. Meanwhile, Peter, Paul and Mary sang against war and social injustice through soulful words and music.

* * *

Moments later, Mark McKenna entered the house. Rainwater dripped from windbreaker jacket and baseball cap. Outside, a streak of lightning illuminated the darkness of night, followed by the explosive rumble of thunder.

Mark was alarmed by the injuries scattering Marty's legs, along with the bump where Turtlehead nailed him with the plastic conduit. "*Whew!*" he breathed, as he removed the windbreaker. "I'm so glad you're here, Marty! I half-way expected to hear about you lying in a gutter someplace, or lying dead in the morgue!"

"Mark," whispered Marty, gazing at his brother through teary eyes.

"You okay, Marty?" inquired Mark, kneeling at his brother's feet. "Did you?... Did you win?"

"Fuck yeah," assured Marty, smiling tenderly. "I a'ways win."

"What about Billy's games?"

"In that box." Marty motioned outside. "On the porch."

"Brace yourself," warned Mark, softly patting Marty's knee. "Mom's in the hospital."

"What?" Jennifer and Marty cried out, in unison.

"How?" begged Jennifer, as Marty quivered in fear.

"Lance..." Mark swallowed. "Lance beat the hell out of her, this afternoon."

"Motherfuckin', cocksuckin' son of a bitch!" cursed Marty, hopping to his feet and running toward the door.

Mark and Jennifer stopped Marty, and forced him to sit back down.

"The cops have already apprehended Lance!" said Mark. "There's no reason to..."

"I don't give a fuck if he ends up in San Quentin with Johnny Cash!" screamed Marty. "Or in Alcatraz escapin' with the *Clint*! I'm gonna kill the son of a bitch, Mark! I'm gonna kill 'em!"

"Mom's all right!" claimed Mark. "Lance knocked her around pretty good, but..."

"Fuckin' bastard!" shrieked Marty. His anger wasn't entirely aimed at Lance, but at himself as well. No matter. Marty would never, could never, let Lance off the hook for what he did to E. Yet, was he also to blame? Arguably, had Marty not beat the hell out of Lance earlier, then maybe E wouldn't be in the hospital now.

It had been a long day, and Marty was exhausted. His entire body hurt from the pounding he took from the Dirtbag and Turtlehead, before he turned the tables and pounded on them. His fever had returned, as his thoughts remained cluttered and chaotic, at odds with themselves.

Marty wasn't only concerned with E. Was he still "good" with Kris? Or were they no longer an item? Fear of losing Kris' love and favor were impossible to endure. Marty thought he'd never make it on his own, without Kris there as a friend, a companion, and confidante and, in time, as a lover.

Fuck, man.

What have I done? What the fuck have I done? Am I all alone in this cruel, fucked-up world?

Oh fuck, man.

Marty concealed his face under both hands, then released a sad, mournful cry. Jennifer leaned over to kiss his teary cheek.

"It's okay," said Mark. "Mom... Mom's just in the hospital overnight... or two nights at the most! They're just making sure she's all right."

"I'm sorry, Mark," wept Marty.

"What do you have to be sorry about?" asked Mark.

"I shouldn't o' beat hell outa Lance!" sobbed Marty. "I shouldn't o' done half the things I done today! Son of a bitch!"

"Lance had it coming," said Mark. "He always had it coming. As far as what you done... Well, shit. Guess you just can't help yourself, Marty. You're gonna do exactly what you're gonna do, that's all. That's what you get for being 'Marty'. What? What else can I expect from my favorite brother?"

Marty sniffled as he looked deep into Mark's eyes. His throat tightened, and he struggled to get the words out. "Am I really your favorite?" he whispered.

"I got it good," laughed Mark, also overwhelmed with emotions. "I got two favorite brothers! Ones Patrick...and the other one's named *Martin!*"

19

Aunt Barbara had treated Billy, Patrick, and Kris to a meal at the local *McDonald's*.

It was a laid-back, enjoyable evening. Barbara allowed the younger boys to dominate the conversation. The two lads enthusiastically yammered on about gaming, the *Marvel Cinematic Universe*, and *Disney*.

Barbara smiled as she listened intuitively. She wasn't actually into superhero movies and had no interest, whatsoever, into gaming. She usually only watched independent and foreign-language films, and listened to Golden Oldies from the 60s, 70s, and 80s. Even then, she treasured the younger boys' company so much she bought them both double-servings of hamburger and fries.

Kris said little. He merely nibbled at this food and stared vacantly at the rain and traffic outside. His mind wasn't on blockbuster movie franchises. He was trapped by fear and nagging insecurities concerning his own life, his future, and his prospects in a crazy, unpredictable world.

Mostly, he fretted over Marty McKenna.

The last Kris saw Marty, the little hooligan had beaten up Turtlehead. Once Edith McCleary caught him spitting on Turtlehead, Marty told everyone to do something which is physically impossible, then disappeared in the night.

Kris should've stopped Marty, or at least tailed him. He wanted to believe that Marty would just get lost for a while, go on a potty-mouthed tirade, then eventually return to Aunt Barbara's.

Although Kris worried about Marty, he wondered if it was really worth it.

There were other fish in the sea. Marty may have been Kris' first love. It didn't mean he wouldn't be Kris' only love. What were the odds of Kris and Marty staying together? In time they'd lead separate lives and separate experiences with separate outcomes...seek separate goals and aspirations...fall in love with separate people, and get on with it.

Kris harbored doubts of having a stable future with Marty. After all, there were other fish in the sea. Yet, despite their differences, the only fish Kris imagined hooking his line to was Marty.

Kris shook his head. *Why? Why, oh Lord? Why am I "that way"? Why did you burden me with such challenges? Why, oh Lord? Why?*

And why am I in love with Marty? Of all guys, why Marty McKenna?

"Enjoy your dinner?" asked Barbara, breaking Kris from his self-imposed Hell.

Kris stared blankly at the burger and fries he barely touched.

"If he don't want 'em," asked Patrick, "then can I take 'em?"

Kris sighed, then took a bite of his meal.

"Let's take it to go," suggested Barbara. "It's getting late, and I'm sure Patrick and Billy have to be home, soon. Their folks are worried sick about them."

"Mom ain't," said Patrick. "Her and Lance prob'ly went to some rotten, stupid party, and we won't see 'em for days."

"I just hope Papa don't throttle me for being gone all day!" moped Billy.

"Well, let's hope not," agreed Barbara, leading her three guests outside to a turquoise, *Volvo* station wagon.

Barbara drove along Main Street, humming a Gordon Lightfoot song which played on the car radio. Kris sat next to her in the front seat, staring through the rain-splattered windows. The windshield wipers slapped back and forth, leaving odd reflections upon the passengers' faces. The smell of the burger and fries in Kris' lap enticed Patrick, while reminding Barbara that her nephew was troubled.

The Volvo turned left at Cherry Street, did a right at Madison, then slowly meandered on a one-way street through a quiet, residential area. Billy's home sat near an interstate underpass. A few blocks away, the sounds of a chugging train were loud, deafening, and thunderous.

Billy said his 'goodbyes', stepped outside, and sprinted to his front door. Inside, his family watched *The Outlaw Josey Wales* on *TCM*.

The *Volvo* soon reached the McKennas' trailer. The porch light was on. However, no one was home. Patrick went inside to find the place damp, musty, uninviting, and cold. He had no desire to spend the evening there, alone, and went to spend the night at Aunt Barbara's.

Minutes later, Barbara pulled the car into her driveway. Everyone bailed out and made a beeline to the living room. There, they found Mark, Jennifer...and Marty.

"'They're coming to get you, Barbara'," greeted Marty, with a silly grin.

His eyes then met Kris'. No one said a word.

Barbara and Patrick took off their jackets and sat down. Meanwhile, Kris and Marty engaged in a bizarre, awkward staring contest. For the exception of Patrick, everyone was concerned on how the two boys handled their reunion.

Finally, Marty leaped from the wicker couch, sprinted toward the door, and embraced Kris. Without hesitation, Kris and Marty locked lips in a long, passionate kiss.

"Faggots," whispered Patrick, in disgust.

Mark and Barbara smiled in approval. Meanwhile, Jennifer had her doubts whether Kris and Marty's relationship would last. She kept her silence. If nothing more, Kris and Marty had someone to lean on... for the time being.

Once they broke free, Kris looked Marty in the eyes and said, "We have to talk."

"And there's a million things I wanna tell you," Marty said, his raspy voice cracking.

Kris glanced at Barbara, seeking permission to go to his bedroom, where he and Marty could speak in private.

"See you in the morning," said Barbara, making herself at home on the beanbag chair.

Kris slowly led Marty to the hallway. He turned, smiled, and wished everyone a pleasant evening.

The others responded in kind.

Kris and Marty entered the bedroom. They locked the door behind them, then sat down on Kris' bed. Without asking to do so, the two threw their arms around each other, kissed, and made out for several minutes. On occasion, they'd whisper, "I'm sorry," or "I love you," then smooch again. Marty ran his fingers through Kris' dishwater blonde hair. Kris

                    Doug McKim

placed one hand on Marty's thigh, the other around his shoulders.

"I'm sorry," spoke Marty, softly rubbing his hand against Kris's face. "Sorry for what I done at the bookstore. Sorry for everything I said and done to hurt you… Sorry for puttin' you through hell, and… and…" Marty wiped away the tears streaming down his cheeks. "I love you, Kris! … I love ya!"

It was a turn-on to see Marty so vulnerable and emotional. Marty was gorgeous in his long-sleeved tee and gym shorts. Still, Kris was fearful and alarmed by the countless abrasions throughout his body.

Marty was kind of cute in a rugged, scruffy sort of way. Kris thought back to that morning when he walked into Marty's bedroom to find the numbskull with his shorts down to the ankles, blatantly revealing his "full glory". No doubt about it, Marty was handsome, clothed or naked. But would he stay that way, assuming he kept fighting? Or would be evolve into a ragged, worn adult, beaten down by the injustices of life and the toll it takes on everyone? Was Marty's youthful appearance enough to maintain Kris' love and need for him?

Kris frowned. He had to have a stern, no-nonsense talk with Marty. Kris only hoped he had the nerve, the courage, and abilities to get his words out. "Marty," he said, praying to speak his mind without stammering or stuttering. "I love you. I love you, more than you will ever know."

"Love ya, too," said Marty.

Kris sighed. "But, Marty… Sometimes, I just don't get you."

Marty grasped Kris' hand, in a plea to never let go.

"I just don't get your anger," said Kris, "your bad language, and those… *things* you say and do to hurt me!"

Marty inadvertently giggled, knowing it was the wrong thing to do. He found no humor in this situation, whatsoever. He suspected that Kris was about to give him the same going over that Jennifer had meted him, earlier.

"What's so funny?" snapped Kris. He was torn between forgiving Marty for most everything, slapping Marty's face off, or throwing his ungrateful ass to the pavement.

Marty smirked. He more he fought an urge to laugh, the harder it got not to. No matter what, Marty couldn't hold back the annoying cackles spilling from his mouth.

"Marty!" shouted Kris.

"I can't help it!" giggled Marty.

Kris pulled his hand away from Marty's, crossed both arms, and pouted. What was the point? What reason did he have now to love Marty?

Marty McKenna?

Kris sought to deny his attraction to Marty, realized that it was in vain, and dreaded realizations that he was forever trapped by his infatuations with the dumb kid. He loved Marty, was in love with Marty, and found him unbelievably attractive, despite the bumps, bruises, and gashes on his beautiful young body.

Damn it.

Kris' attempts to communicate with Marty had blown up in his face. He was screwed…unbelievably screwed. Kris loved Marty, yet found him so frustrating and aggravating!

"Kris," whined Marty. By now, he had stopped laughing. His grin was replaced by a sad, pathetic, puppy-dog expression. "Kris, if ya fuckin' leave me, I'll kill myself!"

Kris' eyes widened.

"I can't live without ya!" sobbed Marty. "I know I been real shitty to ya. Fuck, man! I been real shitty to everybody!"

What hostilities Kris may have felt toward Marty now gave way to forgiveness. "Marty…"

"I'm shittiest to the ones I love the most!" bawled Marty, lowering his face in shame and embarrassment.

"You sure don't love the Dirtbag or Turtlehead," commented Kris. "And you been real shitty to them, too."

Marty smirked, even in sorrow. He rested his head against Kris' chest. The constant beating of Kris' heart was comforting and assuring. "Kris," he said. "My mom's in the hospital!"

Kris gasped. "*What?*"

"Lance put Mom in the fuckin' hospital!"

Kris forgot all about his worries and doubts, and instead concentrated on Marty's. "What happened?" he begged.

"Fuck if I know," sighed Marty. "Mark told me. Lance put Mom in the fuckin' hospital, the son of a bitch."

"Where's Lance now?"

"The cops grabbed 'em. Too bad. I'd rather kill 'em, myself."

Kris gave Marty a hug.

The two teens now shared a priceless moment of solitude. No words were spoken. Kris and Marty simply realized they needed each other.

Their mutual attachment spoke more truth than words ever could.

Kris took in a deep breath, then released it in a sigh. He resigned himself to the knowledge that he was stuck with Marty, and Marty was stuck with him. They were together, like it or not. Even if their romance failed, they'd stay close friends, the sort of friends one may call on the phone sit down over beer or coffee, and confide in during the toughest of times. If not lovers, then at least friends, to the very end.

"My life's fucked up, Kris," whined Marty. "I'm a shitty fuckin' person. So fuckin' shitty! Everything's so fucked up and shitty."

"It doesn't always have to be that way," said Kris, examining Marty's unruly hair, his thin build, and finally his sinewy yet smooth legs...splendid to behold even if they were beaten and bruised.

Kris was lucky to have Marty in his life. Even then, their relationship came with demands and conditions. Marty had looked after Kris in the past. It was obvious that Marty also required a keeper, someone to prevent him from getting into trouble. Marty instilled Kris with confidence. Kris was there to stop Marty from taking on the entire world, armed only with a wild temper and bad language.

Kris thought back to that afternoon in the OK Corral, with Barry and Abigail Thatcher. He imagined the life that the elderly had together, in their years of marriage. Surely, it must have been wonderful! In all likelihood, however, there were still hardships. Did Barry and Abigail ever separate during that time, or even cheat on each other? Were there ever periods of instability and violence, or painful and harsh words? Did either ever come home late after a drunken night in a tavern, do something to trouble their partner, then spend the next few days regretting it? Did Barry and Abigail ever once question their love and affection for each other?

Did Kris and Marty ever stand a chance? Would Marty remain ruggedly handsome? Or did it even matter? Perhaps Marty was only handsome in Kris' eyes. And was it realistic for Kris to expect Marty to curb his anger, stubbornness, and stupidity?

Kris prayed that Marty would finally grow up, then find better solutions to handle problems. He also hoped Marty would take on more responsible and respectable. Above all else, Marty had to stop fighting! Was that too much to ask for? After all, Marty was Marty.

Would Kris learn to accept Marty, despite his shortcomings? And would Marty accept Kris, simply for being Kris? More important, was Kris willing to accept himself, along with "the way he was"?

Finally, Kris prayed that God accepted his love for Marty McKenna, the same way He accepted Barry and Abigail's love and commitment.

"Marty," sighed Kris, rubbing Marty's thigh. "Please don't ask me why, and please don't ask me to explain. But I love you, and I can't live without you."

"Love ya, too," said Marty, deeply moved and touched.

"Guess this means we'd better learn to live together, or die apart," said Kris, anxiously. "Okay, Marty? *Okay*, Marty?... *Okay?*"

Marty smiled as he kissed Kris' lips. "*Okay!*"

20

"Hey, Jen," Mark said to his girlfriend, while sitting at Aunt Barbara's dining room table. "What do you think if we just stay in Grangeford and enroll at *NOU*?"

It was now 9:30 in the evening. The rain, thunder, and lightning outside had finally stopped. The clouds were dissipating, and a full moon illuminated the night sky. Still, the wind was heavy, as the air grew cold and frigid. Grangeford was destined for a June frost.

Patrick turned on the TV, and enjoyed an anime cartoon. Everyone else sat at the dining room table, drinking Henry Weinhard's and Black Butte Porter. Patrick relaxed on the beanbag chair, watching Tokyo get blown to bits by an unknown, celestial force. Minutes later, he fell asleep.

Mark was obviously worried, since he arrived at Barbara's to announce that E was in the hospital. He smiled warmly, and kept the conversation hospitable. Even then, his worried eyes and expressions told of unspoken anxieties and tension. This wasn't lost on Jennifer or Barbara.

Finally, Mark repeated, "Hey, Jen. What do you think if we just stay in Grangeford and enroll at NOU?"

NOU was *Northern Oregon University*, one of the few colleges in that region of the state. It sat on the outskirts of town. Years before, it was regarded as a laughing stock. However, recently NOU had broadened its curriculum, updated its aging facilities, and became a reasonable alternative to "big city" colleges and universities.

Jennifer glared at Mark in disbelief and shock.

For the longest time, Mark and Jennifer had discussed an exit strategy out of Grangeford. They planned on relocating either to Eugene or Corvallis, then get an education at Oregon State or the University of Oregon. The two would then make a living in the arts, and live happily ever after. They'd be out of the OK Corral, and the hell out of Grangeford.

"It won't be such a big move," mumbled Mark.

"I thought we both agreed to give the Corral our two-week notices in the spring, then high-tail it out of here!" snapped Jennifer.

"Something...came up," sighed Mark, evasively.

"'Came up'?" questioned Jennifer. Little-by-little, she got fed-up and tired of life in her old hometown, and yearned for that which lie beyond the evergreen forests, high-mountain desert, and granite peaks surrounding Grangeford. She wanted what many of her high school classmates now enjoyed - broader horizons, better opportunities, and grand adventures. She sought a "new and improved" Jennifer English, living the sweet life and doing what she what she always wished to do, with the man of her dreams... a "new and improved" Mark McKenna.

Jennifer also wanted Kris in a more accepting community. She spent too many sleepless nights, worried about his happiness and safety. Increasingly, she found herself counting backwards on an arbitrary calendar, when her and Mark left Grangeford. And now Mark wanted to stay! What the hell was that? Just what the hell was that?

"Well?" demanded Jennifer.

"Might as well tell us, honey," urged Barbara. "One way or the other, we'll get the truth from you. Jennifer and I are women, and you're outnumbered."

"I spoke with the doc this evening," said Mark, on the verge of weeping. "Mom's doc, y' see... and..."

"What's wrong, Mark?" begged Jennifer.

"Yes," said Barbara. "Please tell us."

Mark shot a quick glance at Patrick, making sure the boy was asleep. "Mom went to see the doc, sometime last week," he said, reluctantly. "I... I didn't know anything about it. I doubt if Pat or Marty know anything, either." His voice cracking, he announced, "Mom's liver is failing."

Barbara and Jennifer were speechless.

It took everything for Mark to get the words out. "From what I heard, her liver's shot... had it. Sounds to me like..." The emotions nearly proved too great. Mark wiped his teary eyes, yet mustered the courage to go on.

"Mom's about to cash out," he whispered. "She's a goner."

Jennifer embraced Mark, as Barbara tightly clutched his hand.

"It doesn't fucking surprise me!" shouted Mark, sadness giving way to anger and hostility. "The way Mom's always carried on, it surprises me she didn't keel over, long before this!"

"Oh, Mark," wept Jennifer. "I'm so sorry!"

Mark gritted his teeth, struggling to get tough about it. If nothing else, at least he could stand on his own two feet. He was plagued by uncertainty, not for himself, but for those dearest to him.

"Is there anything the doctors can do for your mom?" inquired Barbara.

"Hell, I dunno," groaned Mark.

"But I feel so terrible, hon," cried Barbara, wishing there was something, *anything*, she could do to help.

"No need to lose sleep over me!" laughed Mark, despite himself. "I been paying the fucking bills around the house. What bill haven't I paid, over the past two years or so? What lazy ass have I supported, just to see her running around, getting drunk, getting stoned, getting laid? Me? What the hell, I'm fine! It ain't me I'm worried about. It ain't even Mom I'm worried about, and it sure as hell ain't Lance!"

Once more, Mark looked at Patrick, sound asleep on the beanbag chair. He then shot a glance down the hall at Kris' bedroom, where Marty was.

Mark and Jennifer had long planned an exit strategy out of Grangeford, and make new lives for themselves. Mark believed that the two owed themselves happiness, prosperity, prospects and promise, beyond serving food and drinks at a greasy spoon. However, he would never, could never, abandon his own kin, who were blameless for the fix they were in. Not only was he obligated to Jennifer, but for those who needed him the most.

Those who now needed him, more than ever!

"Who I'm really worried about," whispered Mark, nervously, "are Pat and Marty."

21

"I didn't ask if you wanted to 'fuck', Marty," said Kris, in the darkness of his bedroom. "I asked if you wanted to make *love*."

As Mark informed Jennifer and Barbara of E McKenna's dire situation, Kris and Marty vowed to make a lasting commitment to each other, prior to turning off the lights and going to bed.

Kris practically dropped onto his bed. He was totally drained. The weather had gotten colder outside, and the bedroom felt damp and chilly. Kris reached over, turned the thermostat up a notch, and yawned. He heard Marty undress from across the room.

Kris stretched his aching back, slipped off his shoes and socks, then slipped out of his blue jean shorts. This left him only in a long-sleeved tee-shirt and skivvies. He got under the blankets, then rested his head upon a soft, fluffy feather pillow.

"G'night, Kris," said Marty. "Love ya, man."

"Good night, Marty," answered Kris. "I love you, too."

Both boys reached out to touch each other's fingers. They clasped hands, and held on for several seconds.

"Love ya," repeated Marty, with a sincerity he hadn't felt or spoken in a very long time.

"I love you, too," said Kris, pulling his hand away from Marty's. "See you tomorrow."

Kris then heard the springs of Marty's bed rattle, as a pale silhouette approached him. "Scoot over," said Marty, lifting the blankets to welcome himself into Kris' bed.

"*What?*" shrieked Kris.

"Scoot over," repeated Marty, making himself at home next to Kris.

Kris' heart skipped a beat, as he felt Marty's warm body pressed against his. He wondered, and feared, what Marty had in mind. It was as much a mystery, a secret and an enticement. "What?" questioned Kris, unsure whether to greet Marty's arrival, or protest it.

Marty threw his arms around Kris, and kissed him on the cheek.

Kris embraced Marty, just to get yet another surprise, equally exciting and scary. "You're nude, Marty!" he shouted. "Marty, you're *nude!*"

"Don'tcha think I know that?" commented Marty.

Panic collided with unspoken yearnings. Kris was thrilled and troubled by thoughts sprinting through his mind. Perhaps this was the night, the very night, that he and Marty finally took their love much further.

Kris debated on whether he was ready to have sex with Marty... while debating whether he'd ever be ready. He uttered a prayer to God Almighty, seeking approval for what might soon occur. And if God refused to grant permission, would He still forgive Kris for possessing weaknesses as seeking love, giving love, and needing to be loved? Needing to be loved by Marty McKenna... while giving himself over to Marty McKenna.

Am I ready? Will I ever be ready?

I do want this...

Don't I?

"It ain't what ya think," said Marty. "I was too fuckin' cold and lonely over there, and I just thought.... Ya don't mind, do ya?"

"No," gulped Kris. "I... I don't mind."

"It's just that..." Marty's tone grew apologetic. "It's just that I wanna be with ya. It don't mean we gotta do that 'nasty', if ya don't wanna."

"It's okay," said Kris, a sense of relief conflicting with 'what if?' "I do want you with me, Marty."

Marty kissed Kris.

"Are you okay?" asked Kris, divided between what was right verses what was best, verses "am I ready?"

"Whadda ya mean?" asked Marty.

"You smell like salve and medicine. I... I'm just worried about you, that's all."

"I ain't dead, yet."

"Yet."

"Don't worry," laughed Marty. "I'm too damn dumb and Irish t' die."

Kris wrapped his arms around Marty. He caressed Marty's back and shoulders, then dared to slide one hand down to his partner's bare bottom, an impulse leading to....

Kris began to sweat, and his heart beat rapidly. Breathing got short and shallow. Love, lust, doubts, fear, guilt, shame, denial, and pleasure warred for dominance. Needs and desires overwhelmed Kris, along with responsibilities and obligations in waiting for the right time.

Was this the right time?

His first time had to be special! No way should it be meaningless, crass, or vulgar... a *wham-bam* sort of event. Was that too much to ask for, especially from Marty McKenna?

"Marty?" Kris whispered in his partner's ear. "Will you make love to me?"

"*Huh?*" shouted Marty.

Kris nearly withdrew the question, but it was too late now. "Will you make love to me?" he whispered, revealing anxiety in a jittery voice.

Marty giggled. "You sayin' ya wanna fuck?"

"I didn't ask if I wanted to 'fuck', Marty," sighed Kris. "I asked if you want to make *love*."

"You mean right now?"

"No!" yelled Kris. "When we're dead and buried!"

Silence wedged the two teens. Kris suddenly remembered the condom that Aunt Barbara gave him earlier, the same condom in the pocket of his blue jean shorts... the condom he hoped to use, should a need arise. "We don't have to go all the way," he suggested, nervously.

"What if we can't help ourselves?" questioned Marty, also stricken with fear. A snicker slipped from his mouth. "I mean...what if everyone hears us going at it in here?"

"How will they know?" asked Kris, increasingly more tense.

"Aw, c'mon Kris!" laughed Marty. "I've seen enough fuck films to know how loud they get when they're doin' the old 'fuck and suck'. All that moanin' and groanin' and gruntin' and pantin'!"

"*Marty!*"

"*Ugh.... Ah.... Oh...*" Marty started, hoping his voice carried into the dining room. "*Ugh.... Oh.... Ugh.... Oh.... UGH.... OH.... UGH.... OHH...*" he continued, consciously louder, and louder, and louder. "***UGH.... OHH.... UGH.... OH.... WHOA, WHOA, WHOA, WHOA....***

AHHH!"

Then, in a high-pitched shriek, he added, "*EEEEHHH!*"

"Marty!" whispered Kris, frantically. "*Stop!*"

"What's wrong?" laughed Marty.

"Why does it always have to be so dirty with you?"

"It ain't dirty t' me! It's only dirty to other people! Can you imagine the bedsprings rattlin' up and down, up and down, while we moan and groan and grunt and scream?" Marty giggled. "Pretty soon, we'll both be squealin' like pigs!"

"Damn you, Marty!" cursed Kris. "Would you rather we go at it in some dark, filthy alley?"

"Well, kinda. Might be a lot more private."

"I don't get you, Marty," commented Kris, in disgust and frustration. "Honestly, I just don't get you, at all!"

Whether he admitted it or not, Marty was also intimidated by thoughts of his first time. Did he also want it, from Kris?

Well... did he?

"'*A minstrel boy to the war is gone*'," sang Marty, seemingly unaware. "'*In the ranks of death ye will find him*'..."

"It's just that..." Kris searched for the right words. "It's just that...I love you, more than anything! Please, Marty? Will you make love to me?"

Marty said nothing. He simply glanced at a digital clock, hanging from a nearby wall.

9:53 pm.

"Please?" insisted Kris, showering Marty's face with kisses. "Do you want to make love?"

"I dunno," said Marty, slowly pressing himself to Kris' warm body. "Do *you?*"

THE END

ABOUT THE AUTHOR

Doug McKim has worked as a dishwasher, a janitor, a journalist, a prep cook, a deli clerk, a mentor, a tutor, a volunteer for economic and community development, a caregiver, and a grave digger. He has a degree in History from Eastern Oregon University.

Originally from Halfway, Oregon, McKim spent a year in Tennessee before settling in La Grande. He is the author of five books: ARE YOU MAN ENOUGH (2010, co-authored with Richard McKim), JUST PLAIN OLD JEREMY (2012), ONE DAY IN THE LIFE OF MARTY McKENNA (2013/2023), LOVE, DEATH, AND ART (2017), and HARVEY MADDEN (2022).

Visit the author's website at dougmckim.com.